Library
Brevard Junior College
Cocoa, Florida

A
TARPAULIN MUSTER

A
TARPAULIN MUSTER

BY

JOHN MASEFIELD
(1878-1967)

Short Story Index Reprint Series

BOOKS FOR LIBRARIES PRESS
FREEPORT, NEW YORK

First Published 1907
Reprinted 1970

INTERNATIONAL STANDARD BOOK NUMBER:
0-8369-3677-9

LIBRARY OF CONGRESS CATALOG CARD NUMBER:
73-132120

PRINTED IN THE UNITED STATES OF AMERICA

TO
H. G. B.

CONTENTS

CHAPTER		PAGE
I	Edward Herries	1
II	A White Night	29
III	Big Jim	37
IV	El Dorado	45
V	The Pirates of Santa Anna	60
VI	Davy Jones's Gift	67
VII	Ghosts	75
VIII	Ambitious Jimmy Hicks	83
IX	Anty Bligh	91
X	On Growing Old	100
XI	A Memory	108
XII	On the Palisades	115
XIII	The Rest-house on the Hill	123
XIV	Gentle People	130
XV	Some Irish Fairies	138
XVI	The Cape Horn Calm	148
XVII	A Port Royal Twister	156
XVIII	In a Fo'c'sle	164
XIX	The Bottom of the Well	171
XX	Being Ashore	179
XXI	One Sunday	187
XXII	A Raines Law Arrest	194
XXIII	The Schooner-man's Close Calls	201
XXIV	The Yarn of Happy Jack	210

I

EDWARD HERRIES

"Only death adds to our length; nor are we grown
In stature to be men, till we are none."
An Anatomy of the World.

EDWARD HERRIES, the poet, rose from his chair, and looked through the window over the darkening valley. The moon had risen over the tree-tops, and the yews made black patches here and there in the mass of trembling branches ridging the hill. He flung back the curtain, so that he might see better; and the moonlight, falling upon him, made yet more pale the paleness of his refined face, now wrung with sorrow. He took one of the silver candlesticks and held it so that the light might fall upon a portrait hanging in the window-nook. It was the portrait of a woman a little older than himself; and one had but to see the confident poise of the sweet head and the firm red line of the lips, and the delicate sharp cutting of the chin, to know that she was one of those queenly women before whom the hearts of the weak and of the strong are as dust upon the road. Edward Herries looked at the picture for a long time, and sighed and bit his lip. "She was right," he said sadly; "she was right. I am not the man for her. I am too goody-goody. She wants a man with more devil in him."

The room was very silent, save for the ticking of a clock. It was a sombre chamber, lighted by the fire and by four candles. The candles guttered now and then as the wind raised the blue curtains and let them fall again. Very far away a church bell tolled the hour and a dog barked, making echoes. Herries sat at the table and covered his eyes with his hands, thinking of the alert, confident, conquering beauty who was passing like a queen, even then, with her court about her, in the great house a few miles away, where the hall shook with the riot of the dance. "Four years," he said sadly; "I have loved her for four years." He placed the portrait in front of him and looked at it again. He thought of the times when he had seen her look like the portrait: wondering a little at the blindness or frailty of the painter, who had seen only that one look, marked only that one passing

beauty, from love's feast and beauty's mirror, so
queenly decked in the woman's face, for any
man with eyes or passion. He had often seen
her look like that, he thought. She had a way
of looking up like that from her work, or book;
and then her lips moved just like that at the
beginning of a smile. If he had been a painter,
he thought, he would have painted her with her
hair loosed; she had glorious hair; and with
the one wrist turned back, as he had seen it once,
showing the lovely arm almost to the elbow. Or
he would have painted her on horseback, galloping at a fence, as he had seen her once; or as
she had stood once under a trailing rose, in
blossom, pulling on the long green riding gloves
which she had won in a bet from one of the
many moths who fluttered about the fire of her
beauty. Then he fell to thinking, with bitter-
ness, of the man who would win her. He called
over the names of the confident, raffish, handsome youths, who fetched and carried for her,
and lost money to her at cards, and bought rare
flowers for her in the winter time, and rode with
her through the countryside, and danced with
her in the winter dances in the halls of the great
houses. She was too noble a woman, he

thought, to take one of those young men; though every one of them (he told them over one by one, weighing their virtue) had some point of manliness, some trick or grace of carriage, or confident surety of address, which himself lacked and longed for. She would dangle those handsome lads for a year or two, and then other passions, or the business of the world, would shake them from her, and they would forget all about her, and burn her withered roses (once the spoils of golden hours) if they ever turned them up among the litter of rubbish; among the letters and spoils of youth, tossed aside in boxes and forgotten for years.

He felt sure that the man who married her would be an elderly, mature man, a soldier or statesman, grave and politic; who would marry her for her beauty and fresh sparkling charm. He would be polite to her (this husband), with a cold, stately politeness, till some heavy tomb, with a heavy epitaph, concealed him from admiring relatives. She was made for a more lovely life than that, he thought. The fancy came to him, as of late it had often come to him, that perhaps her gaiety and gallant carriage were but blinds to the true woman; and that that seeming heart of courage would be glad to falter and loiter; and that a little tenderness, even a little sadness in the voice, might set the old manner shaking, and show the true woman underneath, of grave heart and noble pride, beautiful exceedingly, glad to lay by the mask. He thought tenderly for a few moments, of life with her, and of the many gentlenesses and unselfishnesses, undreamed of by most men, for which marriage gives the opportunity. He thought of her in sickness, in sadness, in possible trouble; and it was a bitter pill for him to think that it would be denied to him to comfort her, or to help her, even if he knew; when she had passed to the keeping of the old soldier, white like his honour, infirm like his science, who tottered and menaced in the young man's fancy, darkened by his present trouble.

There was a paper lying on the table; the young man picked it up. It was written upon in his beautiful script; its very erasures were refined. The writing was an unfinished sonnet, full of a haunting melancholy, which pleased the young man as he read it over:

I saw that sacred wood where Beauty's rose —

He sighed plaintively, altering " that " to

"the," after some deliberation. "She was right," he said sadly. "I'm too goody-goody. The only thing I'm fit for is poetry. She wants a man with more devil in him." For a moment he thought that it would be glorious to make his life, as it were, an altar, ever smoking with sacrifice; a ritual ever beautiful with her worship; living aloof and consecrate, in beautiful emotion, praising this woman in his art; so that her name might be a torch, a holy fire, to the lovers of all time. That would be beautiful, he thought; but only for a moment. The sonnet before him was not a perfect sonnet; the love was well; one or two lines were beautiful, there was a fine image; but the couplet spoiled it; it rang thin, did that concluding couplet. "I'm no good even at poetry," he sighed. "It takes a man even to write a sonnet — a man with devil in him."

I saw the sacred wood where Beauty's rose —

He altered "the" to "that" again, with delicate fineness, so as to make no blot upon the script. "Beauty of the world," he said, "Oh burning beauty of the world. Would I were a violet in the grass, hidden among the dead thorn leaves, that your passing foot might crush me.

The thrush in the may blossom is happier than
I," he said, " for he sees you going lightly
among the flowers, among the golden bells of
the flowers, among the pale stars of the flowers,
among the passionate crimson flowers, and the
flowers that are white like your soul. Oh
beauty, oh beauty of the world," he said, " you
are like the sun upon the flowers, like the sun in
April. The hedges bud with their fresh green
shoots, there is blossom on the hedges. The
brooks chatter down the meadow; and the
blackbird sings. It is April when you are passing. There is April in my heart, oh beautiful
woman, when I see your beauty brightening the
world like the sun.

" I am no good to you," he added, sighing.
" I'm a lame crock, my sweet. I am a little dust
for you to tread on; a little violet for you to
wear and forget; a song sung softly to you, to
pleasure you for five minutes." He repeated
the phrase several times, as though it gave him
importance. " I'm a lame crock, indeed," he
said. " I blush when I pass two men at a street
corner." He leaned his head upon his hands,
and thought of the quiet, ordered, beautiful
life, which had made him so shy, so self-con-

scious, so unfit for mixture with the clumsy boors of the world of the unthinking. He had always lived a secluded, sheltered life, among many books, and in great cities, where a man's neighbour is his enemy, or rival. He had but to raise his eyes, and to look about him, to see, as it were, the symbol of his life in the gear he had gathered for his room. There were the four silver candlesticks, and the heavy blue curtains; the case of books, in their bindings of parchment and leather, with their broken clasps and backs; the Spanish swords over the fireplace; the three Venetian goblets, the bowl of flowered bronze, heaped with gems, beads of blue and red, amber pellets, and some old silver coins from the Greek islands. "Life has been this to me, all along," he said. "Good Lord, this has been life to me; this room. Wherever I have gone, in Paris, in Leyden, in Venice, in Rome, in Padua, I have had this room. I have been shut in by these four walls, lit by those four lights, guided by all that rubbish on the shelf, amused by all those gimcracks on the mantel." The pageant had gone by him, the god had gone by him, tossing his laurels, as he sat blinking by candlelight at the little Venetian Petrarch in italic type. Life had meant nothing more to him than this room, these gauds, the manuscripts in the lavender, the dusty gems in the bowl. All the beauty and strangeness of the world had been before him; but he had seen it from a comfortable window, never from the eyes of men and women, fiery with passion, or a divine hope.

And of his friends, of the young men who had been boys with him, who hung at the beck of the beautiful woman, glad to beg roses from her, and to beg for them like so many puppies. One of them was a soldier, who had been in three fights, and had run through a trooper in a skirmish. He walked with swing, with style, as though the world were free quarters to him. He had a scarlet cloak, which set somehow over the sword, so that his whole figure had a gallantry, a brave rakish decision, which made way for him in crowded roads, and won him the respect of servants. Another was of the King's court; and had gone in the train of the ambassador to Paris, where he had fought a duel for the love of a lady. Another was a sportsman, who could ride, run, wrestle, or fence with any man in England. A fourth was a breaker of hearts, a lover of women, whose old age would be haunted by the eyes of beautiful women, beseeching and appealing. A fifth, who could sing delicately, was excellent at all games of skill, at cards, at quoits, at bowls; so that in that little court he was a desired knight, to whom many roses were given. They were all his inferiors, he felt. Their brains were the brains of healthy dogs or horses; but he had only to join their company, in that low room so often hallowed by his love, to feel that they had a virtue which would never be his: a decisive, manly style; a knowledge of life and of the world; which carried them through crises enough to destroy him. They were, if he had but seen as much, the world. He was one of those who are not of the world. He was one of those shy, self-conscious souls, never at ease, never happy, in the world, but living (the immortal part of them) in Paradise, and trying always to drag their unwilling bodies across the heavenly frontier. "My life has been a failure," he cried. "I have created a life for myself, and it crumbles like clay, now that it is put to the test. I have lived among shadows and essences; among ghosts, among the dead, among memories. I have bowed my mind among poems, and in the beautiful thoughts of men who lived greatly. And all the time the pageant has been passing, the horses trampling, the music shaking the air, the eyes of the dancers burning, the passion awake in the heart, the tumult throbbing in the blood. All the time, men have gone by me to the battle; women have plucked at my sleeve, desiring my love; there has been wine poured out in the cup, and music playing me to the dance. And I, that have striven to love nobly, to make my heart a sweet sacrifice to the woman I love, have made myself a weak, stooping, blushing failure, whom women can only pity or despise; but never love."

He thought for a moment of another sonnet he had written. It was, as he told himself, the golden feather — the plume — of his beautiful youth and of his love. It began —

> When, as a serf in her dear heavenly court,

and it had given him comfort many times, when he had seen her jesting among her young men. She was greater than that, the sonnet said; that was only the dress, or manner, or outward semblance of her — that light, laughing woman.

In herself, the sonnet said, she was a queen, a spirit, a bird of heaven, a creature of heavenly blessing. Her mask of confident gaiety was nothing but a pretty screen before heaven itself. He repeated the sonnet; but the assurance of his most perfect moment could not be brought back by its shadow. "Ah yes," he said; "so I thought. But I thought then that she might love a poet. I know now that she will only love a man. I know her now. I know that sweet woman to her very heart's blood now. I love her now. I know her. I know her value. When I wrote that, I loved only my Idea of her." He was pleased by the phrase, and repeated it. "I loved only my Idea of her." The thought flashed through his mind, that the Idea is the divine truth; but he was lecturing, not conversing with himself, and the thought died in his brain. "I loved only my Idea of her," he repeated. "That lover is dead. Now I love her as she is, for what she is, and now it is my task to make myself worthy of her, to make myself a man, who am now only a lover."

He unlocked a little copper box, which stood upon the mantel, holding nearly everything which made life precious to him. There were

two little books which she had given to him:
a Lovelace and a Donne, both sacred books.
There was a packet of letters, laid carefully in
lavender. There was a handkerchief, believed
to be hers, which he had found in the garden.
There was a little book, in green leather, containing all that he could remember of her, her
visits and amusements, her spoken words.
There was his mother's Prayer Book, with a
little of her writing in it. In the Prayer Book
were some flowers, very brittle and brown, which
had each its memory of her, dead though they
were. He turned them over sadly, almost with
tears, with a kind of awe, as though the giver
were dead. "Violets," he said sadly, "violets
— little white violets. She wore you in her
belt, dear blossoms. Oh, holy woman, oh, lovely
creature of God, I would my blood were flowers
to fling at your feet." He remembered picking
the white violets; he remembered where they
grew — on a sunny bank, outside a coppice;
where, if one lay still, in the sun, in the sweet
scent, the rabbits would come nibbling, almost
within reach. He had picked a sprig of mistletoe on the same day, he remembered. It lay
there, too, though broken, and very dry. That

had been a golden day — a day to remember — the day that he picked the violets. She had been thoughtful that day, and he had read poetry to her — Donne's poetry — until the passion of that great heart had almost moved him to tears. He had always kept the anniversary of that day, worshipping its relics with a ritual of poetry and sweet feeling. It was in April; and he would always remember April; he prayed that he might die in April; for that sweet day's sake. He repeated the name April, as though the lovely name would bring about him the loveliness of the spring, with its rooks cawing home, its daffodils, its corn springing green from the earth, its primroses in the dewy valleys. She had meant the whole of April to him, she moved his blood like the spring; beauty quickened in his heart at the thought of her, as the young grass quickens in April, as the bud in the hawthorn breaks into its white blossom.

He handled his relics reverently, almost with tears, with an infinite awe and humbleness. He felt that he stood on one of the heights of life, that his love made him almost holy, that his thoughts were as armed spirits guarding her from evil. Then, as before, he was troubled by that doubt of his, that he had loved only his Idea of her; that he had worshipped the idea, not the woman; that he had now to fill that lack in himself which made him, after these four years, no worthy mate for her. He bowed his head upon his hands as he remembered his last talk with her; as she sat among her court, laughing and jesting. He blushed to think of his distress among those young men, who sat there with such easy good humour, so ready with their silly chatter; so skilled in retort; so quick to make her laugh. He remembered a jest of hers, a light thing enough; but done with such a grace, with so much of the woman's nature in it, it had had the effect of genius. He bowed his head again, with the thought that all character is a manifestation of genius, and that the building up of such a woman, out of a child, out of a schoolgirl, was a divine work of genius, that she was a divine thing, radiant and peerless; her wit and beauty being alike sparkles from the heavenly fire. "I loved only my Idea of her," he repeated. "Now I love her as she is, for what she is, and now it is my task to make myself worthy of her, to make myself a man, who am now only a lover.

"What shall I do?" he cried. "What shall I do? I have lived among essences, among memories: and if I stay here, among these books, I shall go on as I have lived, a lover, a shadow, unstable as flame." A vision shone for a moment in his mind, of the laughing, radiant beauty, in her maddest mood, tossing comfits to her courtiers, for them to catch in their mouths, like dogs. "Ah yes," he sighed.

> "When thou hast stayed and done thy most,
> A naked thinking heart, that makes no show,
> Is to a woman but a kind of ghost.
> How shall she know my heart?"

"I must go away to some less ordered life, to a world where a man may live by what he is. A man must not live by what he feels, nor by what he has read, but by the will, the courage, the wit of the swordsman who fights among many edges." He snapped to the lid of the little copper box, feeling that he was shutting away from himself a part of his life which was beautiful and sacred, like a night of summer, at full moon. "I have lived in moonlight," he thought. "My world has been white like moonlight, and pure like moonlight. Now over the valley comes the sun, golden like corn, bounteous as July.

EDWARD HERRIES 17

Now, my beloved, my beauty, my share of God upon earth, your knight goes out into the sun." He leaned his head over the portrait, and kissed the sweet face which smiled out at him.

"Ah, my beloved," he said. "It may be that I shall die abroad. I may never see you again, dear beauty. Dear woman, I may never see you again. But if I die, dear heart, down in the dust I shall thrill, I shall tremble, at the thought of your kindness, at the thought of your beauty, your beauty that makes you like fire, like God. Ah, if I die, far off, among strangers, my soul will travel the forest, and cross the seas, and flutter to your feet, dear woman, like a moth at the flame. It may be that I shall know your heart, when my body is dead, and it may be that I may shield you, dear love, if you are in trouble or in danger."

There were tears in his eyes as he stopped speaking. He placed the miniature in an inner pocket, and turned to go. The old woman, who kept house for him, would see to everything, he thought; and he left the candles burning as a symbol of his heart, if not from carelessness; and so he passed down the stairs, to the stables where his horse stood saddled.

As he rode through the little town, so quiet under the moon, he wondered at the beauty of the night. " Beauty is the shadow of God," he said. " All lovely things are as feathers fallen from His wings, brightening the air. A beautiful face is a letter in God's alphabet. To think of a beautiful face is to have one's prayer answered." An owl called from the wood; for now he was clear of the town; and at the cry of the bird, so haunting, so full of suggestion, he reined in. There before him was his lady's house, standing great and ghostly in the moonlight, with its one fir tree shaking its darkness against the stars. There was a light in the room, high up; and he watched it for many minutes, with feelings which were like prayers, if incoherent. "Ah, dear woman, dear woman," said his passionate heart, "may my prayers be a shield to you. May my spirit be about your spirit. May my prayers be as a sword before you, dear thing of God, dear wonder." His head bowed upon his chest, the reins slipped from his fingers; his tears were falling. " My heart is full of your beauty," he cried; " my heart is a cup flowing with your beauty; the angels and the saints drink of my heart in

the courts of heaven." He could not say more,
for the words choked him. He looked sadly at
the lighted room, a look of farewell, then the
image of her face swam into his mind, in a blinding mist, in an agony. He shook his horse into
a walk, and rode on, sobbing, through the
summer night, so sweet, so full of odours, so
noisy, with the nightjars and the owl's hooting.

It was autumn, five years later, that he came
home again. He rode up from the little seaport, one rainy day in October, when the woods
were grey with cloud, and the ways melancholy
with the dripping of drops. Little gusts of
wind set the boughs shaking as he rode; and at
every gust drops pattered hurriedly, in a
rhythm almost musical, quick to cease. He had
changed much in the five years; and none of
those who passed him, bowed under their cloaks,
hurrying through the wet, knew him for Edward
Herries. Now and then he drew rein under
some sheltering bough, to look at the well-
known country, beautiful, even in its autumn
melancholy, with memories of the woman he
loved. There was the hill, dark with yew

trees, where she had hurt her foot, when walking with him, one winter morning. There, at the corner, she had galloped past him one windy March day, when the beauty of the wild weather seemed to have passed into her blood. Under the wood, where the rolls of cloud hung, they had looked for primroses; and that had been a good day, a day of joy, that day in the spring, when they had looked for primroses. He remembered the dress she wore, and the way her face was raised to him. He remembered the beauty of her look, as she knelt for a moment, under the hazel boughs, on the green moss of the clay, to pick from a plant full of blossoms. Somehow the memories were strange. They stirred him, they were fire to him; but they were not as they had been. He was remembering his youth: that was it: he was remembering his youth; the woman was only one of the colours in the picture.

He had changed much in the five years. He had been far from books, roving the world. He had grown sturdier, coarser, more self-assertive. He had been in battles and marches, at the sack of towns, at the boarding of ships at sea. He had many violent memories, memories of war and of anger, black and savage, to lay by his memories of her beauty. When he thought of her, his thoughts were tinged with these new memories; his mind had been altered by them. The horse slipped; he swore at him as he pulled him up, thinking that the oath might have made a difference, had she heard it, years ago, in the old days.

The old woman who kept house for him was there. Nothing had changed. The pigeons still ruffled and sidled; they still tumbled in the air; they still cooed drowsily. There were pools in the gravel just where there had been in the past, in rainy weather. The little leaden Cupid still bowed over the fountain. The aspen still trembled and trembled, like a guilty thing, like a wild thing, like an unhappy thing. It was all as it had been — the books, the swords, the silver candlesticks; the gems and amber in the bowl. There was his friend, his friend who had been a soldier, come to welcome him. He hadn't changed either; he was the same or seemed so. They sat down to dinner together in the old room hung with so many portraits, dark with so many memories.

After dinner they took their wine to the fire and sat there, drinking; and as they drank, Herries found himself wondering at his friend, once so alert and lively, but now so dull. "I am this man's master," he thought. "This is a common creature. He has lived his youth. I am only now come to my youth." "Ah yes," said his friend. "You see my father died, and so I settled down. Oh, I didn't tell you — I'm married. Got two children. You may remember Polly Gray." Herries had a memory of a red-faced giggling lady; he thought with sadness of the lives of the children under such parents, of the lives of the parents, of the passing of the flower of beauty. He took a sip of wine and stirred the fire. "How's the great house?" he asked casually. "Is *she* there still?" Yes, she was there still. No, she hadn't married; she had lost her looks a little; grown paler. "Ah well," said Herries sadly, "we all do that." After that they talked of horses. "A good thing your going away, Herries," said his friend. "You've lost your nonsense. You used to be always reading poetry." "Yes," said Herries, "I have lost my nonsense. I have lost it indeed.

"Man," he continued, "life is nonsense. It is a flower, and we give it for an idea; it is an idea, and we give it for a flower. I have trodden my life in the dust, and the dust chokes me." The friend would not drink any more wine, and Herries was too stiff with his ride to set him home.

It was on a melancholy morning that Herries went to the great house. He went half angrily, irritated by the memories of the past; and half expectantly, as touched by them. If his old love were kind, he thought, it would be very blessed and very beautiful. Yet the old life was dead to him. He could not live the old ordered, secluded life any more. He had been a wild bird, and no cage would ever again hold him. He wondered that she should have borne with him in the old days. "I was a whining puppy," he said savagely; and as he said it a phrase from a sonnet rose up, like a straw, in the eddy of his mind. "Puppy," he repeated, blushing, "I was callow in those days. How could she have borne with me?" It is not good to know the answer to that question. When we know the answer to that question we have done with youth.

He did not remember the servant who opened the door to him; but his heart beat more quickly at seeing the old armour on the panels; and the cracked Zucchero, in its carved frame, just as it had been in the past. He lingered a moment in the hall, thinking of the many times he had imagined his return; and of the many times he had gone to that house in the spirit, during his five years of exile. The blood quickened in his veins for a moment, as his soul framed the likeness of his old love as she had been, but with the lovely face abashed, the red lips trembling, before the perfected lover, tried in the world's fire, now worthy of her love. The servant returned, asked him to follow, preceded him. They walked through dark rooms, along corridors, under portraits with grave eyes, portraits of ladies long dead, and of men long forgotten.

"Beauty and virtue can neither die nor be forgotten," he had once proudly thought, in passing those faces. The thought came back to him now; he remembered the epigram he had made, and repeated it. "The beauty of a woman, the virtue of a man, are parts of God, often the only parts we men and women see. A woman's beauty is eternal. It can never fade. It becomes a part of the beauty of the world. No sentiment," he said to himself sharply, checking the poetry. "Passion is of heaven or of earth. Sentiment lives in limbo. I have won clear of limbo." The servant opened the door and spoke his name.

The room was unchanged, as far as he could see. There was the tapestry of the finding of Moses; there was the drawing, in red chalk, of the woman of Samaria; nothing had changed. He was disappointed somehow; and the first greeting, so long looked for, so long practised in the spirit, was over before its significance came home to him. He had thought that the touch of her hand would be sacramental, a rapture, a removal of the seals. The fine, delicate hand merely touched his, and then it was withdrawn. He was conscious of an effort to remember whether he had really touched her. He was disappointed with the greeting. It had been a common thing, after all; after all his dreams. He was disappointed with the face of his old love; his homecoming had been a failure. She was beautiful still; for her beauty was that intellectual beauty which changes little from

childhood to old age. The sweet face had
grown, perhaps, paler; the eyes, in that light,
seemed darker; the expression was changed and
calmed; the hair was heaped in a new fashion.
He remembered the old, quickly changing, eager
look, the flushed cheek, the bright eyes, which
had moved him so strangely in the past; he was
angry that they were no longer there; he was
vexed that her voice had none of its old laugh-
ter. He was conscious that he, too, had altered. The woman beside him, whose eyes were
so dear and yet so strange, was surely aware of
that. He, too, had altered. He felt that the
woman judged him; and that she, who, in the
past, judged nothing, ate, now, only of the
golden kernel, drank only of the hidden waters;
lived only in an inner temple builded of intellectual beauty. As he spoke to her he thought
of his roving in the world, and of the Spanish
women he had kissed. It seemed to him that
those women sat at his side, with roses in their
hair, and their lips still tempting his. It seemed
to him that she saw them. It seemed to him
that he walked in the temple of her mind for a
moment, a smirched and booted figure, and that
those women walked with him, laughing, rose-

crowned, flushed, spreading defilement. He had thought, of old, that this woman would be won by mastery, by conquest, as it were by storm. He saw now that she could be won only by service, by humbleness, by beautiful sacrifice. From her eyes, so dear and lovely, a lovely spirit looked. Her spirit was a white bird nested among golden branches. He longed to kneel to her, to cry to her, to put from him the stains of the five years. He felt like a bird beaten from covert, with a broken wing. His five years had not helped him; his five years had rubbed off the golden plating, which had hidden his common metal from the eyes of the world. The assurance of the common nature, the assurance of the beast that lusts and snarls, was no fit plume for the knight of such a woman. She had walked the fire. That lovely heart had achieved the heavenly alchemy; the bird in her sang; the perfect clay had burned into the divine gold. From the ashes of her conquered self rose up the flowers. She was a heavenly citizen, this beautiful lady. The blood came and went upon his cheeks, and the words choked him, as he looked upon her. He, too, long ago, made holy by his love of her, had lived in paradise. He had given his Idea for a common flower of the hedge, while the golden rose blossomed by him. He went out from the great house, into the autumn day, ashamed and humbled; the sword of her beauty hacking the brambles from his soul. "I am fallen among the brambles," he sighed. "I am blackened and ashamed." His mind burned with the memory of her beauty. Her beauty was still a beacon to him. By the light of her beauty he could see the briars and brambles lying in a tangle of thorns to shut him from the golden door.

II

A WHITE NIGHT

SOMETIMES, when I am idle, my mind fills with a vivid memory. Some old night at sea, or in a tavern, or on the roads, or some adventure half forgotten, rises up in sharp detail, alive with meaning. The thing or image, whatever it may be, comes back to me so clearly outlined, under such strong light, that it is as though the act were playing before me on a lighted stage. Such a memory always appears to me significant, like certain dreams. I find myself thinking of an old adventure, a day in a boat, a walk by still waters, the crying of curlews, or the call of wild swans, as though such memories, rather than the great events in life, were the things deeply significant. I think of a day beside a pool where the tattered reeds were shaking, and a fish leapt, making rings, as though the day were a great poem which I had written. I can think of a walk by twilight, among bracken and slowly moving deer, under a September moonrise, till I am almost startled to find myself indoors. For the most part my significant memories are of the sea. Three such memories, constantly recurring, appear to me as direct revelations of something too great for human comprehension. The deeds or events they image were little in themselves, however pleasant in the doing, and I know no reason why they should haunt me so strangely, so many years after they occurred.

One winter night, fourteen years ago, I was aboard a ship then lying at anchor in a great river. It was a fine night, full of stars, but moonless. There was no wind; but a strong tide was running; and a suck and gurgle sounded all along the ship's length, from the bows to the man-catcher. I had been dancing below-decks by lamplight with my shipmates, and had come up for a turn in the air before going to my hammock. As I walked the deck, under the rigging, with my friend, a pipe sounded from below. "Away third cutters." I was the stroke oar of the third cutter, and I remembered then that a man had been dining with the captain, and that he would be going ashore, and that he would need a red-baize cushion to sit upon, and a boat-rug to cover his knees. I ran below to get these things, and to haul the boat alongside from her boom. As I stepped into her with the gear, I heard the coxswain speaking to the officer of the watch. "It's coming on very hazy, sir. Shall I take the boat's compass and the lantern?"

I noticed then that it was growing very hazy. The lights of the ship were burning dim, and I could not see a long line of lights, marking a wharf, which had shone clearly but a few moments before. I put the cushion in the stern-sheets and arranged the rug for the visitor, and then stood up in my place, holding the boat to the gangway by the manrope. The coxswain came shambling down the ladder with his lantern and compass. The officer in charge of the boat came after him, with his oilskins on his arm. Then came the visitor, a tall, red-haired man, who bumped his hat off while coming through the entry-port. I could see the ship's side and the patches of yellow light at her ports, and the lieutenant standing on the gangway with his head outlined against the light.

We got out our oars and shoved off through the haze. The red-haired man took out a cigar and tried to light it, but the head of the match came off and burnt his fingers. He swore curtly. The officer laughed. "Remember the boat's crew," he said. In the darkness, amid the gurgle of the running water, over which the haze came stealthily, the words were like words heard in a dream. I repeated them to myself as I rowed, wondering where I had heard them before. It seemed to me that they had been said before, somewhere, very long ago, and that if I could remember where I should know more than any man knew. I tried to remember where I had heard them, for I felt that there was but a vague film between me and a great secret. I seemed to be outside a door opening into some strange world. The door, I felt, was ajar, and I could hear strange people moving just within, and I knew that a little matter, perhaps an act of will, perhaps blind chance, would fling the door wide, in blinding light, or shut it in my face. The rhythm of rowing, like all rhythm, such as dancing, or poetry, or music, had taken me beyond myself. The coxswain behind the backboard, with his head nodding down over the lantern, and the two men beneath him, seemed to have become inhuman. I myself felt more than

A WHITE NIGHT

human. I seemed to have escaped from time. We were eternal things, rowing slowly through space, upon some unfathomable errand, such as the Sphinx might send to some occult power, guarded by winged bulls, in old Chaldea.

When we ran alongside the jetty, the haze was thick behind us, like a grey blanket covering the river. I got out with the stern-fast, and held the lantern for the visitor to clamber out by. The officer ran up the jetty to a little shop at the jetty head where the ship's letters were left. The visitor thanked me for my help, and said " Good night," and vanished into the mist. His steps sounded on the slippery stones. They showed us that he was walking gingerly. Once he struck a ringbolt and swore. Then he passed the officer, and the two exchanged a few parting words. I thought at the time that the casual things in life were life's greatest mysteries. It seemed as though something had failed to happen; as though something — something beautiful — had been kept from the world by some blind chance or wilful fate. Who was the red-haired man, I wondered, that we, who had come from many wanderings and many sorrows, should take him to our memories for ever, for no shown cause? We should remember him for ever. He would be the august thing of that white night's rowing. We should remember him at solemn moments. Perhaps as we lay a-dying we should remember him. He had said good night to us and had passed on up the jetty, and we did not know who he was, nor what he was, and we should be gone in a few days' time, and we should never see him again. As for him, he would never think of us again. He would remember his dented hat, and his burnt finger, and perhaps, if it had been very good, his dinner.

When we shoved off again for the ship the haze was so thick that we could not see three feet in front of us. All the river was hidden in a coat of grey. The sirens of many steamers hooted mournfully as they passed up or down, unseen. We could hear the bell-signals from the hulks, half a mile away. Voices came out of the greyness, from nowhere in particular. Men hailed each other from invisible bridges. A boat passed us under oars, with her people talking. A confused noise of many screws, beating irregularly, came over the muffled water. They might have been miles away — many miles —

or hard upon us. It is impossible to judge by sound in a haze so thick. We rowed on quietly into the unknown.

We were a long time rowing, for we did not know where we were, and the tide swept us down, and the bells and sirens puzzled us. Once we lay on our oars and rocked in a swell while some great steamer thrashed past hooting. The bells beat now near, now very far away. We were no longer human beings, but things much greater or much less. We were detached from life and time. We had become elemental, like the fog that hid us. I could have stayed in the boat there, rowing through the haze, for all eternity. The grunt of the rowlocks, and the wash and drip of the oars, and the measured breath of the men behind me, keeping time to me, were a music passing harps. The strangeness and dimness of it all, and the halo round the coxswain's lantern, and the faces half seen, and the noises sounding from all sides impressed me like a revelation.

"Oars a minute," said the coxswain. "There's the fog-bell."

Somewhere out of the grey haze a little silver bell was striking. It beat four strokes, and paused, and then again four strokes, and again a pause, from some place high above us. And then, quite near to us, we heard the long, shrill call of a pipe and a great stamp of feet upon hatchways.

"Good Lord! we're right on top of her," said the officer. "I see her boom. Ship ahoy!"

"Is that you, Carter?"

We bumped alongside, and held her there while the officer and coxswain ran up the gangway with the letters. We laid in the oars and unshipped the rudder, and a man came down the gangway for the red-baize cushion and the rug. "Hook your boat on," said the officer of the watch.

That is one of the memories which come back to me, when I am idle, with the reality of the deed itself. It is one of those memories which haunt me, as symbols of something unimagined, of something greater than life expressed in life. Why such a thing should haunt me I cannot tell, for the words, now they are written down, seem foolish. Within the ivory gate, and well without it, one is safe; but perhaps one must not peep through the opening when it hangs for a little while ajar.

III

BIG JIM

ONE afternoon, many years ago, I was in a Western seaport, with a day's " liberty " to do what I liked. There were few attractions in the seaport except seamen's dance-houses and drinking dens, so I pushed inland, up some barren sand-hills, into the wilderness. High up among the hills I came to a silver mine, with a little inn or wine shop close to the shaft, and (more strange in that desert) a sort of evergreen pine tree with some of its branches still alive. There was a bench near the door of the tavern, so I sat down to rest; and I remember looking at the russet-coloured earth from the shaft and wondering whether silver mining were hard work or not. I had had enough of hard work to last me through my time. There was a view over the sea from where I sat. I could see the anchorage and the ships and a few rocks with surf about them, and a train puffing into the depot. A barquentine was being towed out by a little dirty tug; and very far away, shining in the sun, an island rose from the sea, whitish, like a swimmer's shoulder. It was a beautiful sight, that anchorage, with the ships lying there so lovely, all their troubles at an end. But I knew that aboard each ship there were young men going to the devil, and mature men wasted, and old men wrecked; and I wondered at the misery and sin which went to make each ship so perfect an image of beauty. As I sat thinking I heard voices inside the tavern, and a noise of crying — the high, one might almost call it griefless, crying of a native woman. Some one came to the door and looked at me once or twice; but I felt this rather than saw it, for my back was to the door and I did not care to look round. Presently I stood up and went into the tavern, to a curious company.

It was a rather large, bare drinking bar, with an earthen floor and adobe walls. The bar was made of a few deal planks nailed to some barrels. Behind it there were some shelves of bottles and a cask or two, and a few mugs, pannikins, and cigar boxes. It was like most low drinking shops; but it was perhaps a shade more bare than the general run. What interested me was the company.

As I entered I noticed that they all looked at me rather hard, and then looked at each other with quick, questioning glances. They were not a difficult crowd to place. They were English and American merchant seamen who had deserted their ships and come mining for a change. But from the way they looked at me it was plain that there was something wrong, and the something was a dead body lying in a corner, half covered by a woman's skirt. By the body, a half-naked woman crouched, wailing in a high, shrill key, which was somehow not at all affecting, as it did not seem to have a passion in it. The body was that of a big, handsome man, evidently the woman's lover. It gave me a kind of awe when I saw that he had a moustache but no beard, for I knew then that the man had been a lover of women; because no man would trouble to shave in such a place without that spur to his vanity. Something told me that the man had died a violent death; but in that country such deaths were common. One of the seamen came up to me and served me with a pannikin of wine; he seemed to be the proprietor. "It was a fight," he said simply, seeing me look at the body. "This morning," he added, "a Chilanean done it." "Who was he?" I asked. "They call him Big Jim," he answered. "He was a big feller, too; an Englishman, I guess. A miner." "He swallowed the anchor," said another seaman. "He come here in a barque," said a third. "They got scrapping," said the fourth. "Over the gell, they got scrapping. Der Chilanean give 'im just one lick, an' Jim quit. There's the knife done it." He jerked his head towards the corner where the body lay; and there, on the mud floor, was a common vaquero's dagger, with a handle stuck about with silver knobs, and a broad, curving, pointed blade. "That was the knife done it."

By and by another miner came loping down the track to the tavern. He rode an old mule, and carried a shovel, which he had borrowed from a friend. He ate some bread, and drank a little wine from the pannikin; and then we all turned out into the air to dig Jim a grave under the forlorn evergreen. It was easy shovelling in that light sandy earth; the grave was soon ready. We went back to the house to fetch the body. The woman was still wailing there in her passionless thin monotone. I believe she hadn't moved since I entered. We had to lift her from the body, for we could not make her understand; she was cowed or dazed; she made no protest, only wailed and wailed like a hurt negro — exactly like a hurt negro; she must have been part negro, a quadroon, perhaps. One of the men asked if the skirt which covered Jim should be buried with him. "Ah, no; leave it for the gell," said one of them; " it's all the skirt she has."

When we laid the body in the grave the sun was about to set; and the burial party seemed touched and unwilling to cover the dead with earth. "I seen him stan' just where he is lying," said one of them. "And I seen him. Only yesterday," said another. "Funny his being dead now and not seeing nothing," said the third. "I guess he didn't think nawthen of dying when he t'r'un out dis morning." "It gives one rather a turn," said the first. "There was Jim. Look what arms he got. He could do a big day's work, Jim could." "Well, he done his last day's work now, Jim has." "Ah," they said, more or less together, "he's touched his pay, Jim has."

Little by little the visitor got some knowledge of Jim as a man and a comrade. He wasn't a drinker, he didn't care for tobacco, didn't use it in any shape. It was girls done Jim. He was a man of education. "If I'd had the education what Jim had I wouldn't be working down no silver mine"— that was what one or two of them told me. "He was a hard case with it," said another; "he never wear more than his oilskins off the Horn. I seen him stand his look-out with only trousers on. I seen it snowing on his chest." "He'd got a fine chest on him, too," said another; "I seen him lift 'alf a ton." "Go on with your 'alf tons," said one; "no man could lift that." "He was strong all right, though," said the first; "'e could carry more than a lanchero." After this some one wondered if the dead man's spirit could see us; for now that the sun was setting the light was beginning to fade, and I know that we all felt the solemnity of life and death, and the certainty that we, too, in time would lie helpless, even as Jim lay. The thought came to us that it would be strange to the body to lie in a grave after so long roving on the world; and to see no fellow-man, to be shut away from companions, after the long life with companions, after the days of love and unselfish tending. It would be strange to the soul, too, we thought, to be loose at last from the old servant and gaoler, and to be like a wild bird again, flying through the world, nesting in no haunt of men, tortured perhaps, perhaps exultant. The general feeling was that God wouldn't be hard on Jim; and the words (whatever they may seem) were tenderly and reverently spoken. To live hard, work hard, die hard, and go to hell in the end would be hard indeed. "It would that," said the others. That was Big Jim's burial service.

We laid a handkerchief over the face, so that the earth might not touch the flesh. Then, with our shovel we covered the body, and heaped the grave with a little pile of earth, and nailed a batten, torn from a packing-case, across the pine tree at his head. We had no pistol for a volley, and it was not for the likes of us to say a prayer, we being still ourselves, and Jim being something beyond us. We stood about the grave a moment, wondering where he came from and whether he had any people. Then we went back to the tavern, to a meal of bread, red wine, and bad dried figs, brought from the sacks and skins which Jim had carried up from town less than a day before.

When I sailed from that port I went aloft to see the last of the silver mine. I could see it, in the clear light, quite plainly; and I could see the one evergreen marking the grave. The chance meetings of life are full of mystery, and this chance adventure, with its sadness and beauty, will always move me. The evergreen must be dead by this time, and perhaps the mine will be worked out and the tavern gone. Big Jim will lie quietly, with the surf roaring very far below him, and no man near him at any time save the muleteers, with their bell-mares and songs, going over the pass into the desert.

IV

EL DORADO

THE night had fallen over the harbour before the winch began to rattle. The stars came out, calm and golden, shaking little tracks in the sea. In the tiers of ships shone the riding-lights. To the westward, where the Point jutted out, the great golden light of Negra winked and glimmered as it revolved. It was a still night but for the noise of the surf, which beat continually, like the marching of an army, along the line of the coast. In one of the tiers of ships there was a sing-song. A crew had gathered on the forecastle head, to beat their pannikins to the stars. The words of their song floated out into the darkness, full of a haunting beauty which thrilled and satisfied me. There was something in the night, in the air, in the beauty of the town, and in the sweetness of the sailors' singing, which made me sorry to be leaving. I should have liked to have gone ashore again, to the Calle del Inca, where the cafés and taverns stood. I should have liked to have seen those stately pale women, in their black robes, with the scarlet roses in their hair, swaying slowly on the stage to the clicking of the castanets. I should have liked to have taken part in another wild dance among the tables of the wine shops. I was sorry to be leaving.

When the winch began to clank, as the cable was hove in, I gathered up my lead-line, and went to the leadsman's dicky, or little projecting platform, on the starboard side. I was to be the leadsman that night, and as we should soon be moving, I made the breast-rope secure, and stood by.

Presently the bell of the engine-room clanged, and there came a wash abaft as the screws thrashed. The ship trembled, as the turbulent trampling of the engines shook her. The bell clanged again; the water below me gleamed and whitened; the dark body of the steamer, with her lines of lit ports, swept slowly across the lights in the harbour. The trampling of the engines steadied, and took to itself a rhythm. We were off. I cast an eye astern at the little town I was so sad to leave, and caught a glimpse of a path of churned water, broadening astern of us. A voice sounded from the promenade deck behind me. "Zat light, what you call 'eem?"

I could not answer. My orders were to keep strict silence. The point of an umbrella took me sharply below the shoulders. "What you call 'eem — zat light? Ze light zere?"

I wondered if I could swing my lead on to him; it was worth trying. Again came the umbrella; and again the bell of the engine-room clanged.

"Are you ready there with the lead?" came the mate's voice above me. "All ready with the lead, sir." "What have we now?" I gathered forward and swung the lead. I could not reach the umbrella-man, even with my spare line. Once, twice, thrice I swung, and pitched the plummet well forward into the bow wash.

"By the deep, eight, sir."

Again the bell clanged; the ship seemed to tremble and stop. "Another cast now, quickly." "And a half, seven, sir." As I hauled in, I again tasted the umbrella, and another question came to me: "What 'ave you do? Why 'ave you do zat?" I swore under my breath. "Are you asleep there, leadsman?" The mate was biting his finger-ends. I sent the lead viciously into the sea. "Quarter less seven, sir." "Another cast, smartly, now." Rapidly I hauled in, humming an old ballad to myself. "We'll have the ship ashore," I repeated. There was a step on the deck behind me, and again came the voice: "Ze man, ze man zere, what 'ave he do? Why 'ave 'e go like so?" "Won't you pass further aft, sir?" said a suave voice. "You're interrup'in' the leadsman." It was one of the quartermasters. Once again the lead flew forward. "By the mark, seven, sir."

There was a pause; then came the voice again: "I go zees way?" "Yes, zees way," said the quartermaster. The steps of the umbrella-man passed away aft. "Zees way," said the quartermaster, under his breath, "zees way! You gawdem Dago!" I could have hugged the fellow.

"What now?" said the old man, leaning over from the bridge. I cast again. "And a half, eight, sir." "We're clear," said the voice above me. "'Speed ahead, Mr. Jenkins." I gathered up my line. The engine-room bell clanged once more; the ship seemed to leap suddenly forward. In a few seconds, even as I coiled my line, the bow wash broadened to a roaring water. The white of it glimmered and boiled, and spun away from us, streaked with fires. Across the stars above us the mists from the smoke-stack stretched in a broad cloud. Below me the engines trampled thunderously. Ahead there were the lights, and the figure of the look-out, and the rush and hurry of the water. Astern, far astern already, were the port, the ships at anchor, and the winking light on the Point. A bugle abaft called the passengers to dinner, and I watched them as they went from their cabins. A lady, in a blue gown, with a shawl round her head, was talking to a man in evening dress. " Isn't it interesting," she remarked, " to hear them making the soundings? " The white shirt was politely non-committal. " Aft there, two of you," said a hard voice, " and trice the ladder up. Smartly now." The lady in the blue dress stopped to watch us.

I did not see the umbrella-man again, until the next day, when I passed him on the hurricane deck. He was looking at the coast through a pair of binoculars. We were running to the north, in perfect Pacific weather, under a soft blue sky that was patrolled by little soft white clouds. The land lay broad to starboard, a land of yellow hills, with surf-beaten outliers of black reef. Here and there we passed villages in the watered valleys, each with its whitewashed church and copper smeltry. The umbrella-man was looking beyond these, at the hills.

He was a little man, this man who had prodded me, with a long, pale face and pale eyes, a long, reddish beard, and hair rather darker, both hair and beard being sparse. He was a fidgety person, always twitching with his hands, and he walked with something of a strut, as though the earth belonged to him. He snapped-to the case of his binoculars as though he had sheathed a sword.

Later in the day, after supper, in the second dog-watch, as I sat smoking on the fore-coamings, he came up to me and spoke to me. "You know zees coas'?" he asked. Yes, I knew the coast. "What you zink?" he asked; "you like 'eem?" No, I didn't like 'eem. "Ah," he said, "you 'ave been wizzin?" I asked him what he meant. "Wizzin," he repeated, "wizzen, in ze contry. You 'ave know ze land, ze peoples?" I growled that I had been within, to Lima, and to Santiago, and that I had been ashore at the Chincha Islands. "Ah," he said, with a strange quickening of interest, "you 'ave been to Lima; you like 'eem?" No, I didn't like 'eem. "But you 'ave been wizzin, wizzin Lima, wizzin ze contry?" No, I had not. "I go wizzin," he said proudly. "It is because I go; zat is why I ask. Zere is few 'ave gone wizzen." An old quartermaster walked up to us. "There's very few come back, sir," he said. "Them Indians——" "Ah, ze Indians," said the little man scornfully, "ze Indians; I zeenk nozzin of ze Indians." "Beg pardon, sir," said the old sailor, "they're a tough crowd, them copper fellers." "I no understan'," said the Frenchman. "They pickle people's heads," said the old sailor, "in the sand or somethin'. They keep for ever pretty near when once they're pickled. They pickle every one's head and sell 'em in Lima; I've knowed 'em get a matter of three pound for a good head." "Heads?" said another sailor. "I had one myself once. I got it at Tacna, but it wasn't properly pickled or something — it was a red-headed beggar the chap as owned it — I had to throw it away. It got too strong for the crowd," he explained. "Ah, zose Indians," said the Frenchman. "I 'ave 'eard; zey tell me, zey tell me at Valparaiso. But ah, it ees a fool; it ees a fool; zere is no Indians." "Beg pardon, sir," said the old sailor, "but if you go up among them jokers, you'll have to watch out they don't pickle you. You'll have to look slippy with a gun, sir." "Ah, a gon," he answered, "a gon. I was not to be bozzered wiz a gon. I 'ave what you call 'eem — peestol." He produced a boy's derringer, which might have cost about ten dollars, Spanish dollars, in the pawnshops of Santiago. "Peestol," murmured a sailor, gasping, as he shambled forward to laugh, "peestol, the gawdem Dago's balmy."

During the next few days I saw the Frenchman frequently. He was a wonder to us, and his plans were discussed at every meal, and in every watch below. In the dog-watches he would come forward, with his eternal questions: "What is wizzin? In ze contry?" We would tell him, "Indians," or "highwaymen," or "a

push of highbinders"; and he would answer:
"It ees nozzin, it ees a fool." Once he asked
us if we had heard of any gold being found
"wizzin." "Gold?" said one of us. "Gold?
O' course there's gold, any God's quantity.
Them Incas ate gold; they're buried in it."
"'Ave you know zem, ze Incas?" he asked
eagerly. "I seen a tomb of theirs once," said
the sailor; "it were in a cave, like the fo'c'sle
yonder, and full of knittin'-needles." "What
is zem?" said the Frenchman. The sailor
shambled below to his chest, and returned with
a handful of little sticks round which some balls
of coloured threads were bound. "Knittin'-
needles," said the sailor. "Them ain't no knittin'-needles," said another; "them's their way
of writin'." "Go on with yer," said the first;
"them's knittin'-needles. Writin'? How could
them be writin'?" "Well, I heard tell once,"
replied the other. "It ees zeir way of writing,"
said the Frenchman; "I 'ave seen; zat is zeir
way of writing; ze knots is zeir letters."
"Bleedin' funny letters, I call 'em," said the
needles-theorist. "You and your needles," said
the other. "Now, what d'ye call 'em?" The
bell upon the bridge clanged. "Eight bells,"

said the company; "aft to muster, boys." The bugle at the saloon-door announced supper.

We were getting pretty well to the north — Mollendo, or thereabouts — when I had my last conversation with the Frenchman. He came up to me one night, as I sat on the deck to leeward of the winch, keeping the first watch as snugly as I could. "You know zees coast long?" he asked. I had not. Then came the never-ceasing, "'Ave you know of ze Incas?" Yes, lot of general talk; and I had seen Inca curios, mostly earthenware, in every port in Peru. "You 'ave seen gold?" No; there was never any gold. The Spaniards made a pretty general average of any gold there was. "It ees a fool," he answered. "I tell you," he went on, "it ees a fool. Zey have say zat; zey 'ave all say zat; it ees a fool. Zere *is* gold. Zere is a hundred million pounds; zere is twenty tousan' million dollars; zere is El Dorado. Beyond ze mountains zere is El Dorado; zere is a town of gold. Zey say zere is no gold? Zere is. I go to find ze gold; zat is what I do; I fin' ze gold, I, Paul Bac." "Alone?" I asked. "I, Paul Bac," he answered.

I looked at him a moment. He was a little

red-haired man, slightly made, but alert and active-looking. He knew no Spanish, no Indian dialects, and he had no comrade. I told him that I thought he didn't know what he was doing. "Ha!" he said. "Listen: I go to Payta; I go by train to Chito; zen I reach ze Morona River; from zere I reach Marinha. Listen: El Dorado is between ze Caqueta and ze Putumayo Rivers, in ze forest." I would have asked him how he knew, but I had to break away to relieve the look-out. I wished the little man good night; I never spoke with him again.

I thought of him all that watch, as I kept scanning the seas. I should be going up and down, I thought, landing passengers through surf, or swaying bananas out of launches, or crying the sounds as we came to moorings. He would be going on under the stars, full of unquenchable hope, stumbling on the bones of kings. He would be wading across bogs, through rivers and swamps, through unutterable and deathly places, singing some song, and thinking of the golden city. He was a pilgrim, a poet, a person to reverence. And if he got there, if he found El Dorado — but that was absurd. I thought of him sadly, with the feeling that he had learned how to live, and that he would die by applying his knowledge. I wondered how he would die. He would be alone there, in the tangle, stumbling across creepers. The poisoned dart would hit him in the back, from the long, polished blow-pipe, such as I had seen in the museums. He would fall on his face, among the jungle. Then the silent Indian would hack off his head with a flint, and pickle it for the Lima markets. He would never get to the Caqueta. Or perhaps he would be caught in an electric storm, an *aire*, as they call them, and be stricken down among the hills on his way to Chito. More probably he would die of hunger or thirst, as so many had died before him. I remembered a cowboy whom I had found under a thorn bush in the Argentine. Paul Bac would be like that cowboy; he would run short of water, and kill his horse for the blood, and then go mad and die.

I was in my bunk when he went ashore at Payta, but a fellow in the other watch told me how he left the ship. There was a discussion in the forecastle that night as to the way the heads were prepared. Some said it was sand;

some said it was the leaf of the *puro* bush; one or two held out for a mixture of pepper and nitrate. One man speculated as to the probable price the head would fetch; and the general vote was for two younds, or two pounds ten. "It wouldn't give me no pleasure," said one of us, "to have that ginger-nob in my chest." "Nor me, it wouldn't," said another; "I draw the line at having a corpse on my tobacker." "And I do," said several. Clearly the Frenchman was destined for a town museum.

It was more than a year after that that I heard of the end of the El Dorado hunter. I was in New York when I heard it, serving behind the bar of a saloon. One evening, as I was mixing cocktails, I heard myself hailed by a customer; and there was Billy Neeld, one of our quartermasters, just come ashore from an Atlantic Transport boat. We had a drink together, and yarned of old times. The names of our old shipmates were like incantations. The breathing of them brought the past before us; the past which was so recent, yet so far away; the past which is so dear to a sailor and so depressing to a landsman. So and so was dead, and Jimmy had gone among the Islands, and Dick had pulled out for home because " he couldn't stick that Mr. Jenkins." Very few of them remained on the Coast; the brothers of the Coast are a shifty crowd.

"D'ye remember the Frenchman," I asked, "the man who was always asking about the Incas?" "The ginger-headed feller?" "Yes, a little fellow." "A red-headed, ambitious little runt? I remember him," said Billy; "he left us at Payta, the time we fouled the launch." "That's the man," I said; "have you heard anything of him?" "Oh, he's dead, all right," said Billy. "His mother came out after him; there was a piece in the *Chile Times* about him." "He was killed, I suppose?" "Yes, them Indians got him, somewhere in Ecuador, Tommy Hains told me. They got his head back, though. It was being sold in the streets; his old mother offered a reward, and the Dagoes got it back for her. He's dead all right, he is; he might ha' known as much, going alone among them Indians. Dead? I guess he is dead; none but a red-headed runt'd have been such a lunk as to try it." "He was an ambitious lad," I said. "Yes," said Billy, "he was. Them ambitious fellers, they want the earth, and they get their blooming heads pickled; that's what they get by it. Here's happy days, young feller."

V

THE PIRATES OF SANTA ANNA

On the coast of Venezuela, not more than thirty miles from Rio Chico, between the mouth of that river and Cape Codera, there is an indentation in the coast, a bay a mile broad, with a sea entrance a hundred yards across. Beyond the beach are the green woods of the tropics, starred with blossoms, brilliant with parrots, musical with the calling of the bellbirds. One may live there for a year and a day, anchored in the blue calm water, yet on the morrow the place will be still new, still alluring, magical. Lying there on a ship's deck, in sight of all that beauty, a beauty a little drowsy and unreal, in the strong sunlight, one believes all the poetry one has ever read. It is difficult to lie there, hearing the water plashing, seeing the still green woods, like a wall of living beauty, without peopling the forest ways with things not quite human. One expects a white Dian in

THE PIRATES OF SANTA ANNA

a leopard skin flying with flushed face after a shy-eyed fawn. Or a centaur in a patch of herbs stamping his hooves, with a little foal at his flank. Or a satyr lying upon moss, cracking nuts with brown teeth and piping in mockery of the bell-birds.

But as a matter of fact no one lives in those woods, except perhaps an Indian who goes thither now and again to kill a parrot with his blow-pipe. The woods have an evil name all along the coast, from Gallinas to the Mangles. They are populous (the tale says) with troubled spirits who go crying there, like the seagulls, all night long under the moon. Up and down the jungle one may hear their voices, when the night has fallen, talking old Spanish or old English or old French in a shrill, excited way that is disconcerting to the hearer. Sometimes, especially at the feasts of the Church, one may hear the woods ring with a pitiful wailing, like the wailing of many wounded hares. Those who put ashore there at these times, if they will but walk the wood at night, may hear voices close beside them, voices full of tears, a thing pitiful to listen to, coming from the poor ghosts who throng the darkness.

Late in the seventeenth century, it seems, there was a Spanish pirate, named Luis of the Scar, who had once been a Church dignitary at Caracas. It is not known why he left the Church, but some think, said my informant, that he fell in love with the daughter of the Governor. It was a pity, too, for he was a learned man, of some wealth, and young. He might have grown to be a bishop of his province and had a tomb, when dead, in the Cathedral. But, loving this lady as he did, he left the Church, asking her to fly with him to one of the islands in the sea, where they might marry and take ship for France. She was a pious lady, bred with much sanctity, so that this proposal from a priest was in the extreme shocking to her. Producing a crucifix, she reminded him of his vows, to which he answered with a passionate Spanish sonnet written by the poet Caral. However, she would none of him, " sonnet nor prose "; and he, poor man, in a fit of anger, went swearing to the quays, where he embarked on a turtler, bound for the Gulf fisheries! He took to drink, while at sea, to beguile the monotony of the voyage and to induce forgetfulness. Off the Isle of Pines he was captured by a pirate, then bound to plunder on the Main. The pirate was a Frenchman who had sailed with Pierre le Grand in the old buccaneering times.

What with threats and some wayward inclination towards that kind of life, Luis became one of the pirate's crew, being initiated shortly afterwards by the old ceremony of the bull's blood. A bull was killed and a copper cauldron filled with his blood, while the pirates, some of whom were Negro, some Indian, some European, stood solemnly in a circle, chanting their sea-songs. By the light of torches Luis was led into the circle, to where the cauldron bubbled above some glowing embers. The chief of the pirates stripped him and flung his clothes among the flames, afterwards splashing blood upon him and giving him a suit of linen clothes that had been dyed red in the cauldron. He then had to drink to the company, *super naculam;* that is, without leaving enough heel-tap to drip more than one drop when the cup was inverted over the thumb-nail. Having passed through the ceremony, he was bidden to select a comrade from among the company, with whom to mess, work, and march until the comradeship should be dissolved. He chose as his comrade an Englishman whose chest was blue with tattoo marks. Then the company went aboard together, singing their songs; and set sail again for the seas with their black banner blowing up above them.

After some years of piracy, Luis rose to be the captain of the gang, and, like so many pirate captains, he strove eagerly to found upon the mainland some little haven of refuge where he might rest after a cruise. He hit upon the little bay we have mentioned, near Cape Codera; for in the woods there he might cut new spars, and in the bay he might careen, without hindrance from the King of Spain. Like the strange French pirate, "Captain Mission," he founded a little township, with a dock, fort, and arsenal, all trim and pretty, where he ruled for several years, amassing much wealth by his profession. But as he grew older, among his wild crew, he became a penitent, and sorrowed for the sins he had committed and the vows he had broken. He called to mind the great church of Caracas, lit dimly by the yellow candles, across the flames of which the incense wreathed its blue smoke. He heard again the chanting of the brothers as they performed the office, after the bell had rung. He saw the little acolytes in their dresses of red and white, and remembered the eastern window, where Santa Anna, the patron, was very glorious in coloured glass.

At last he called his company together and preached to that motley gang as eloquently as in his youth he had preached before his bishop. He told them of their sins and bade them repent of them, begging them to renounce that way of life before it was too late. For himself, he said, he would start to build there some trim chapel to Santa Anna, his old patron, that so he might atone his sins towards her. Those who cared for this world, he said, might take the ships and go, but he begged those who repented to stay to aid the pious work. He so won upon them that not more than twenty of those rough men thought fit to jeer at him. All the others repented with the fervour of primitive people, and the building of the votive chapel began that afternoon. In six months it was completed, painted, beautified, with all manner of little wooden saints upon its gables. Then a fine thought came to Luis (inspired, no doubt, by the great saint), that this chapel should be consecrated by the Bishop of Caracas, at whose white hands (he thought) the company might be absolved of their sins. He wrote a letter to the bishop, reverently making his submission, and begging that a set of men so penitent might be received again into the Church. Several days passed and no letter came in reply, for the bishop's answer took another shape. It came sailing into the bay one morning, a smart frigate of thirty cannon, with the King of Spain's instructions to " destroy all pirates." By the end of the day Luis and his men lay dead. They had been shot by the marines against the wall of the chapel. They were even denied the offices of the frigate's chaplain, so that their poor lost souls now wander in the woods, crying and whimpering like the seagulls. On certain nights, the Spaniards say, they may be seen there in the moonlight, busily gilding an image of Santa Anna designed to hang above the altar. If one listens, it is said, one may hear very faintly, above the noises of the forest, the words of one of the penitential psalms coming like a sigh from the poor ghosts as they work.

VI

DAVY JONES'S GIFT

"Once upon a time," said the sailor, "the Devil and Davy Jones came to Cardiff, to the place called Tiger Bay. They put up at Tony Adams's, not far from Pier Head, at the corner of Sunday Lane. And all the time they stayed there they used to be going to the rum-shop, where they sat at a table, smoking their cigars, and dicing each other for different persons' souls. Now you must know that the Devil gets landsmen, and Davy Jones gets sailor-folk; and they get tired of having always the same, so then they dice each other for some of another sort.

"One time they were in a place in Mary Street, having some burnt brandy, and playing red and black for the people passing. And while they were looking out on the street and turning the cards, they saw all the people on the sidewalk breaking their necks to get into the gutter. And they saw all the shop-people running out and kowtowing, and all the carts pulling up, and all the police saluting. 'Here comes a big nob,' said Davy Jones. 'Yes,' said the Devil; 'it's the Bishop that's stopping with the Mayor.' 'Red or black?' said Davy Jones, picking up a card. 'I don't play for bishops,' said the Devil. 'I respect the cloth,' he said. 'Come on, man,' said Davy Jones. 'I'd give an admiral to have a bishop. Come on, now; make your game. Red or black?' 'Well, I say red,' said the Devil. 'It's the ace of clubs,' said Davy Jones; 'I win; and it's the first bishop ever I had in my life.' The Devil was mighty angry at that — at losing a bishop. 'I'll not play any more,' he said; 'I'm off home. Some people gets too good cards for me. There was some queer shuffling when that pack was cut, that's my belief.'

"'Ah, stay and be friends, man,' said Davy Jones. 'Look at what's coming down the street. I'll give you that for nothing.'

"Now, coming down the street there was a reefer — one of those apprentice fellows. And he was brass-bound fit to play music. He stood about six feet, and there were bright brass buttons down his jacket, and on his collar, and

DAVY JONES'S GIFT

on his sleeves. His cap had a big gold badge, with a house-flag in seven different colours in the middle of it, and a gold chain cable of a chinstay twisted round it. He was wearing his cap on three hairs, and he was walking on both the sidewalks and all the road. His trousers were cut like wind-sails round the ankles. He had a fathom of red silk tie rolling out over his chest. He'd a cigarette in a twisted clay holder a foot and a half long. He was chewing tobacco over his shoulders as he walked. He'd a bottle of rum-hot in one hand, a bag of jam tarts in the other, and his pockets were full of love-letters from every port between Rio and Callao, round by the East.

" 'You mean to say you'll give me that?' said the Devil. 'I will,' said Davy Jones, 'and a beauty he is. I never see a finer.' 'He is, indeed, a beauty,' said the Devil. 'I take back what I said about the cards. I'm sorry I spoke crusty. What's the matter with some more burnt brandy?' 'Burnt brandy be it,' said Davy Jones. So then they rang the bell, and ordered a new jug and clean glasses.

"Now the Devil was so proud of what Davy Jones had given him, he couldn't keep away from him. He used to hang about the East Bute Docks, under the red-brick clock-tower, looking at the barque the young man worked aboard. Bill Harker his name was. He was in a West Coast barque, the *Coronel*, loading fuel for Hilo. So at last, when the *Coronel* was sailing, the Devil shipped himself aboard her, as one of the crowd in the fo'c'sle, and away they went down the Channel. At first he was very happy, for Bill Harker was in the same watch, and the two would yarn together. And though he was wise when he shipped, Bill Harker taught him a lot. There was a lot of things Bill Harker knew about. But when they were off the River Plate, they got caught in a pampero, and it blew very hard, and a big green sea began to run. The *Coronel* was a wet ship, and for three days you could stand upon her poop, and look forward and see nothing but a smother of foam from the break of the poop to the jib-boom. The crew had to roost on the poop. The fo'c'sle was flooded out. So while they were like this the flying jib worked loose. 'The jib will be gone in half a tick,' said the mate. 'Out there, one of you, and make it fast, before it blows away.' But the boom was dipping under every minute, and the waist was four feet deep, and green water came aboard all along her length. So none of the crowd would go forward. Then Bill Harker shambled out, and away he went forward, with the green seas smashing over him, and he lay out along the jibboom and made the sail fast, and jolly nearly drowned he was. 'That's a brave lad, that Bill Harker,' said the Devil. 'Ah, come off,' said the sailors. 'Them reefers, they haven't got souls to be saved.' It was that that set the Devil thinking.

"By and by they came up with the Horn; and if it had blown off the Plate, it now blew off the roof. Talk about wind and weather. They got them both for sure aboard the *Coronel*. And it blew all the sails off her, and she rolled all her masts out, and the seas made a breach of her bulwarks, and the ice knocked a hole in her bows. So watch and watch they pumped the old *Coronel*, and the leak gained steadily, and there they were hove to under a weather cloth, five and a half degrees to the south of anything. And while they were like this, just about giving up hope, the old man sent the watch below, and told them they could start prayers. So the

Devil crept on to the top of the half-deck, to look through the scuttle, to see what the reefers were doing, and what kind of prayers Bill Harker was putting up. And he saw them all sitting round the table, under the lamp, with Bill Harker at the head. And each of them had a hand of cards, and a length of knotted rope-yarn, and they were playing able-whackets. Each man in turn put down a card, and swore a new blasphemy, and if his swear didn't come as he played the card, then all the others hit him with their teasers. But they never once had a chance to hit Bill Harker. 'I think they were right about his soul,' said the Devil. And he sighed, like he was sad.

"Shortly after that the *Coronel* went down, and all hands drowned in her, saving only Bill and the Devil. They came up out of the smothering green seas, and saw the stars blinking in the sky, and heard the wind howling like a pack of dogs. They managed to get aboard the *Coronel's* hen-house, which had come adrift, and floated. The fowls were all drowned inside, so they lived on drowned hens. As for drink, they had to do without, for there was none. When they got thirsty they splashed their faces with salt water; but they were so cold they didn't feel thirst very bad. They drifted three days and three nights, till their skins were all cracked and salt-caked. And all the Devil thought of was whether Bill Harker had a soul. And Bill kept telling the Devil what a thundering big feed they would have as soon as they fetched to port, and how good a rum-hot would be, with a lump of sugar and a bit of lemon peel.

"And at last the old hen-house came bump on to Terra del Fuego, and there were some natives cooking rabbits. So the Devil and Bill made a raid of the whole jing bang, and ate till they were tired. Then they had a drink out of a brook, and a warm by the fire, and a pleasant sleep. 'Now,' said the Devil, 'I will see if he's got a soul. I'll see if he give thanks.' So after an hour or two Bill took a turn up and down and came to the Devil. 'It's mighty dull on this forgotten continent,' he said. 'Have you got a ha'penny?' 'No,' said the Devil. 'What in joy d'ye want with a ha'penny?' 'I might have played you pitch and toss,' said Bill. 'It was better fun on the hen-coop than here.' 'I give you up,' said the Devil; 'you've no more soul than the inner part of an empty barrel.'

And with that the Devil vanished in a flame of sulphur.

"Bill stretched himself, and put another shrub on the fire. He picked up a few round shells, and began a game of knucklebones."

VII

GHOSTS

"Ghosts are common enough," said an old sailor to me the other day, "but they aren't often seen. It's only common ghosts who are seen." The finer spirits may only be seen by spirits as fine as they. The grosser spirits, as of pirates, highwaymen, suicides, or of such men as hack and hew each other in the Sagas, these may be seen by ordinary people, in ordinary moods, in daylight, in the public roads. Most of us have known a haunted house; some of us may know of haunted countrysides, of pools, of woods, of quiet valleys, where immortal things still trouble the peace of mortals. For my own part, I know of a little river running through a wood; and the quiet of its dark depth and the stillness of the watching forest give it an abiding horror, a spirit of its own, terrible and malign. I can never pass by that river or among those quiet trees without feeling that about me are a multitude of spirits —

some, perhaps, compassionate, but most of them evil — who resent my presence there or would make me one with themselves. The river broadens out into a lake beyond the wood, and the lake is haunted. One has but to look at it to see that it is haunted. Evil is stamped on some scenes as upon some faces; and evil is upon that trembling water and crouched in the reeds beside it and in the darkness of its rocks and deeps. A boy once saw what haunted it, and ran home white with fear and foaming at the mouth. He said he saw " a kind of a red wirrim watching him," with one pale, passionless eye, cold and blue, like a March heaven or the eye of an octopus.

"Some parts of the sea are haunted," says the old sailor, "but some parts aren't. It depends where you go. There's some parts is full of spirits, and others without any. They aren't seen much, but sometimes they come aboard ships, but not to hurt. They wouldn't hurt. They might cause dreams and that — nothing to hurt. Charming young ladies, some of them. They wouldn't do a feller any harm." He told me that the early morning is the best time to see them, at a little before turn-to time,

GHOSTS

before the cook has coffee ready. Sometimes —
in fact, most frequently — one does not see
them, but feels them to be about, in the air, on
deck, somewhere. This feeling I have had myself; perhaps most men have had it; a feeling
that there is some one present, dodging about
on the deckhouse, among the boats, on the
booms, or in among the bitts. There is an old
story of a ship which carried an extra hand
who had never signed articles. The crew discovered, when they were in blue water, that one
watch had a man too many. " He was one of
them who wanted a passage," said my friend,
" or perhaps he may have been the Devil.
There's no knowing."

These wandering spirits who come aboard to
cause dreams are sometimes knavish. I know
of a sea captain who dreamed that by altering
his course he would pick up a boat of castaways.
The dream was very vivid, so vivid that he
could see the ax marks along the teak of the
boat's gunnel where they had cut the cover's
lacings. He was much upset by the dream, for
he did not wish to spoil a good passage; yet he
felt that by keeping to his course he might be responsible for the deaths of his fellow-men. Un-

like most captains, he confided in his mate, who was a man of great piety. The mate felt it to be a sign from Heaven. The ship's course was altered, and for the rest of the day she had a man in her top-gallant cross-trees, looking out for any boat or raft of the sort seen in the vision. When it grew dark the captain burned occasional blue lights and fired off his pistol and blew his foghorn. The next morning, when it was plain that there were no castaways, he agreed with his mate that he had done all that was in his power. The ship was brought to her course and continued her voyage, and the whisky which had been uncorked ready for the sufferers, consoled the after guard at dinner.

I once knew a sailor who had sailed in a haunted passenger steamer. She was one of the ships plying between the Plate and Liverpool, but I cannot mention her name, as she is still afloat. She has one peculiarity — a poop as big as the poop of an East Indiaman. On the poop there are many boats, with other clutter, such as skylights and a wheelhouse; but there is free space enough for passengers to play cricket or to dance without breaking their bones. The poop is haunted. The sailor who

GHOSTS

told me of the ghosts was one of the ship's quartermasters. On one passage, when the ship was in the tropics, he had the middle watch below. The " fo'c'sle " (which happened to be aft, under the poop) was stiflingly hot, so that he could not sleep, though the windsails were set and the vessel was going through it at a steady clip. At last he turned out of his bunk, took a blanket and a pillow, and went on deck to sleep. He made up his bed on the poop to leeward of one of the boats, and settled down to rest at about three in the morning, just as the dawn had begun to change the colour of the sky. He did not know how long he slept; but he woke up with a start to see a line of men " brooming down " the poop towards him, with a boatswain in front of them swilling buckets of water on to the deck as they worked aft. He saw them plainly " as I see my dinner on my plate," some three or four yards away, all working hard. They were so near that he sprang to his feet at once, grabbing up his gear lest it should be wetted. He had hardly taken his gear in his hand when he thought, with a shock, that he had overslept himself at least an hour and a half; that it was now half-past five, since they were washing decks; that he hadn't been to muster, and that he would get a bee in his ear, if nothing worse, for going on deck to sleep without leaving word where he could be found. As he got up he saw that the boatswain and the hands took no notice of him, though one of the sweepers looked in his direction. "He was a red-headed fellow," said the quartermaster, "and he'd got a scar across one cheek like he'd been hit by a club; an ugly-looking lad he was. So I knew at once he wasn't one of our crowd. And I saw him as plain as I stand here, and he looked at me; and I saw the boatswain as plain too; I saw him tell the red-headed fellow to heave round on his broom and not go dreaming like a God-send-Sunday fellow. No, I didn't hear him say that; I only seen him. And the fellow he went on brooming down directly I seen him get told. I felt queer all over; it was so natural. I wasn't dreaming. I was awake all right. It was a vision. Or if it wasn't a vision, I'll tell you what it was — it was sent. It was sent as a warning. That red-headed fellow was a warning. Sometime I shall meet that red-headed fellow, and, you mark my words, he'll give me a queer push. So I shall stand from under when I come alongside of him. I'd know him again if I saw him all right. Some day I shall see him." The vision, or warning, or whatever it was kept him awake for the rest of the watch. He went below to the fo'c'sle, having had enough of the poop, and found that he had been asleep hardly more than twenty minutes.

There is something wrong with that poop. It is not a canny place. I know of another queer thing which happened there, and of a man who started up from his sleep beside a boat to prophesy of what should happen to him in a year's time. The prophecy seemed to every one the most crack-brained nonsense; but it was fulfilled exactly, almost to a day, certainly within a week of the time predicted.

But ghosts are common things, commercial things, things which can only squeak and gibber and frighten poor travellers. They are the base ones of the spiritual world. A ship, a beautiful ship, over which the moral virtue of so many men has been awakened, must be peopled by spirits more lovely than red-headed sailors. The lovely bow, which leans and cleaves, slashing the sea into flame, is surely guarded by a presence, erect, winged, fiery, having the eyes and the ardour of one of the intellectual kingdom. At the wheel, the kicking, side-bruising wheel, which takes charge, and grunts, and flings one over the box, there stand for ever those mailed ones, the ship's guides and guards.

VIII

AMBITIOUS JIMMY HICKS

"Well," said the captain of the foretop to me, "it's our cutter today, and you're the youngest hand, and you'll be bowman. Can you pull an oar?" "No," I answered. "Well, you'd better pull one today, my son, or mind your eye. You'll climb Zion's Hill tonight if you go catching any crabs." With that he went swaggering along the deck, chewing his quid of sweet-cake. I thought lugubriously of Zion's Hill, a very different place from the one in the Bible, and the longer I thought, the chillier came the sweat on my palms. "Away cutters," went the pipe a moment later. "Down to your boat, foretopmen." I skidded down the gangway into the bows of the cutter, and cast the turns from the painter, keeping the boat secured by a single turn. A strong tide was running, and the broken water was flying up in spray. Dirty water ran in trickles down my sleeves. The thwarts were wet. A lot of dirty water was slopping about in the well. "Bowman," said the captain of the foretop, "why haven't you cleaned your boat out?" "I didn't know I had to." "Well, next time you don't know we'll jolly well duck you in it. Let go forrard. Back a stroke, starboard. Down port, and shove her off." "Where are we going?" asked the stroke. "We're going to the etceteraed slip to get the etceteraed love-letters. Now look alive in the bows there. Get your oars out and give way. If I come forward with the tiller your heads'll ache for a week." I got out my oar, or rather I got out the oar which had been left to me. It was one of the midship oars, the longest and heaviest in the boat. With this I made a shift to pull till we neared the slip, when I had to lay my oar in, gather up the painter, and stand by to leap on to the jetty to make the boat fast as we came alongside. I have known some misery in my time, but the agony of that moment, wondering if I should fall headlong on the slippery green weed, in the sight of the old sailors smoking there, was as bitter as any I have suffered. The cutter's nose rubbed the dangling seaweed. I made a spring, slipped, steadied myself, cast the painter around

AMBITIOUS JIMMY HICKS

the mooring-hook, and made the boat fast. "A round turn and two half hitches," I murmured, as I passed the turns, "and a third half hitch for luck." "Come off with your third half hitch," said one of the old sailors. "You and your three half hitches. You're like Jimmy Hicks, the come-day go-day. You want to do too much, you do. You'd go dry the keel with a towel, wouldn't you, rather than take a caulk? Come off with your third hitch."

Late that night I saw the old sailor in the lamproom, cleaning the heavy copper lamps. I asked if I might help him, for I wished to hear the story of Jimmy Hicks. He gave me half a dozen lamps to clean, with a mass of cotton waste and a few rags, most of them the relics of our soft cloth working caps. "Heave round, my son," he said, "and get an appetite for your supper." When I had cleaned two or three of my lamps I asked him to tell me about Jimmy Hicks.

"Ah," he said, "you want to be warned by him. You're too ambitious [i. e. fond of work] altogether. Look at you coming here to clean my lamps. And you after pulling in the cutter. I wouldn't care to be like Jimmy Hicks.

No. I wouldn't that. It's only young fellies like you wants to be like Jimmy Hicks."

"Who was Jimmy Hicks?" I asked; "and what was it he did?"

"Ah," said the old man, "did you ever hear tell of the Black Ball Line? Well, there's no ships like them ships now. You think them Cunarders at the buoy there; you think them fine. You should a seen the *Red Jacket*, or the *John James Green*, or the *Thermopylæ*. By dad, that *was* a sight. Spars — talk of spars. And skysail yards on all three masts, and a flying jib-boom the angels could have picked their teeth with. Sixty-six days they took, the Thames to Sydney Heads. It's never been done before nor since. Well, Jimmy Hicks he was a young, ambitious felly, the same as you. And he was in one of them ships. I was shipmates with him myself.

"Well, of all the red-headed ambitious fellies I think Jimmy Hicks was the worst. Yes, sir. I think he was the worst. The day they got to sea the bosun set him to scrub the fo'c'sle. So he gets some sand and holystone and a three-cornered scraper, and he scrubs that fo'c'sle fit for an admiral. He begun that job at three bells in the morning watch, and he was doing it at eight bells, and half his watch below he was doing it, and when they called him for dinner he was still doing it. Talk about white. White was black alongside them planks. So in the afternoon it came on to blow. Yes, sir, it breezed up. So they had to snug her down. So Jimmy Hicks he went up and made the skysails fast, and then he made the royals fast. And then he come down to see had he got a good furl on them. And then up he went again and put a new stow on the skysail. And then he went up again to tinker the main royal bunt. Them furls of his, by dad, they reminded me of Sefton Park. Yes, sir; they was that like Sunday clothes.

" He was always like that. He wasn't never happy unless he was putting whippings on ropes' ends, or pointing the topgallant and royal braces, or polishing the brass on the ladders till it was as bright as gold. Always doing something. Always doing more than his piece. The last to leave the deck and the first to come up when hands were called. If he was told to whip a rope, he pointed it and gave it a rub of slush and Flemish-coiled it. If he was told to broom down the top of a deckhouse he got it white with a holystone. He was like the poet —

Double, double, toil and trouble.— Shakespeare.

That was Jimmy Hicks. Yes, sir, that was him. You want to be warned by him. You hear the terrible end he come to.

" Now they was coming home in that ship. And what do you suppose they had on board? Well, they had silks. My word they was silks. Light as muslin. Worth a pound a fathom. All yellow and blue and red. All the colours. And a gloss. It was like so much moonlight. Well. They had a lot of that. Then they had china tea, and it wasn't none of your skilly. No, sir. It was tea the King of Spain could have drunk in the golden palaces of Rome. There was flaviour. Worth eighteen shilling a pound that tea was. The same as the Queen drunk. It was like meat that tea was. You didn't want no meat if you had a cup of that. Worth two hundred thousand pound that ship's freight was. And a general in the army was a passenger. Besides a bishop.

" So as they were coming home they got caught in a cyclone, off of the Mauritius.

AMBITIOUS JIMMY HICKS

Whoo! You should a heard the wind. O mommer, it just blew. And the cold green seas they kept coming aboard. Ker-woosh, they kept coming. And the ship she groaned and she strained, and she worked her planking open. So it was all hands to the pumps, general and bishop and all, and they kept pumping out tea, all ready made with salt water. That was all they had to live on for three days. Salt-water tea. Very wholesome it is, too, for them that like it. *And* for them that's inclined to consumption.

"By and by the pumps choked. 'The silks is in the well,' said the mate. 'To your prayers, boys. We're gone up.' 'Hold on with prayers,' said the old man. 'Get a tackle rigged and hoist the boat out. You can pray afterwards. Work is prayer,' he says, 'so long as I command.' 'Lively there,' says the mate. 'Up there one of you with a block. Out to the mainyard arm and rig a tackle! Lively now. Stamp and go. She's settling under us.' So Jimmy Hicks seizes a tackle and they hook it on to the longboat, and Jimmy nips into the rigging with one of the blocks in his hand. And they clear it away to him as he goes. And she was settling like a stone all the time. 'Look slippy there, you!' cries the mate, as Jimmy lays out on the yard. For the sea was crawling across the deck. It was time to be gone out of that.

"And Jimmy gets to the yard-arm, and he takes a round turn with his lashing, and he makes a half hitch, and he makes a second half hitch. 'Yard-arm, there!' hails the mate. 'May we hoist away?' 'Hold on,' says Jimmy, 'till I make her fast,' he says. And just as he makes his third half hitch and yells to them to sway away —— Ker-woosh! there comes a great green sea. And down they all go — ship, and tea, and mate, and bishop, and general, and Jimmy, and the whole lash-up. All the whole lot of them. And all because he would wait to take the third half hitch. So you be warned by Jimmy Hicks, my son. And don't you be neither red-headed nor ambitious."

IX

ANTY BLIGH

ONE night in the tropics I was "farmer" in the middle watch — that is, I had neither "wheel" nor "look out" to stand during the four hours I stayed on deck. We were running down the North-east Trades, and the ship was sailing herself, and the wind was gentle, and it was very still on board, the blocks whining as she rolled, and the waves talking, and the wheel-chains clanking, and a light noise aloft of pattering and tapping. The sea was all pale with moonlight, and from the lamproom door, where the watch was mustered, I could see a red stain on the water from the port sidelight. The mate was walking the weather side of the poop, while the boatswain sat on the booby-hatch humming an old tune and making a sheath for his knife. The watch were lying on the deck, out of the moonlight, in the shadow of the break of the poop. Most of them were sleeping, propped against the bulkhead. One of them was singing a new chanty he had made, beating out the tune with his pipe-stem, in a little quiet voice that fitted the silence of the night.

> Ha! ha! Why don't you blow?
> O ho!
> Come, roll him over,

repeated over and over again, as though he could never tire of the beauty of the words and the tune.

Presently he got up from where he was and came over to me. He was one of the best men we had aboard — a young Dane who talked English like a native. We had had business dealings during the dog watch, some hours before, and he had bought a towel from me, and I had let him have it cheap, as I had one or two to spare. He sat down beside me, and began a conversation, discussing a number of sailor matters, such as the danger of sleeping in the moonlight, the poison supposed to lurk in cold boiled potatoes, and the folly of having a good time in port. From these we passed to the consideration of piracy, colouring our talk with anecdotes of pirates. "Ah, there was no pirate," said my friend, "like old Anty Bligh

of Bristol. Dey hung old Anty Bligh off of
the Brazils. He was the core and the strands
of an old rogue, old Anty Bligh was. Dey hung
old Anty Bligh on Fernando Noronha, where
the prison is. And he walked after, Anty
Bligh did. That shows how bad he was."
"How did he walk?" I asked. "Let's hear
about him." "Oh, they jest hung him," replied my friend, "like they'd hang any one
else, and they left him on the gallows after.
Dey thought old Anty was too bad to bury, I
guess. And there was a young Spanish captain
on the island in dem times. Frisco Baldo his
name was. He was a terror. So the night
dey hung old Anty, Frisco was getting gorgeous
wid some other captains in a kind of a drinking
shanty. And de other captains say to Frisco,
' I bet you a month's pay you won't go and put
a rope round Anty's legs.' And ' I bet you a
new suit of clothes you won't put a bowline
around Anty's ankles.' And ' I bet you a cask
of wine you won't put Anty's feet in a noose.'
' I bet you I will,' says Frisco Baldo. ' What's
a dead man anyways,' he says, ' and why should
I be feared of Anty Bligh? Give us a rope,'
he says, ' and I'll lash him up with seven turns,

like a sailor would a hammock.' So he drinks up his glass, and gets a stretch of rope, and out he goes into the dark to where the gallows stood. It was a new moon dat time, and it was as dark as the end of a sea-boot and as blind as the toe. And the gallows was right down by the sea dat time because old Anty Bligh was a pirate. So he comes up under the gallows, and there was old Anty Bligh hanging. And 'Way-ho, Anty,' he says. 'Lash and carry, Anty,' he says. 'I'm going to lash you up like a hammock.' So he slips a bowline around Anty's feet." . . . Here my informant broke off his yarn to light his pipe. After a few puffs he went on.

"Now when a man's hanged in hemp," he said gravely, "you mustn't never touch him with what killed him, for fear he should come to life on you. You mark that. Don't you forget it. So soon as ever Frisco Baldo sets that bowline around Anty's feet, old Anty looks down from his noose, and though it was dark, Frisco Baldo could see him plain enough. 'Thank you, young man,' said Anty; 'just cast that turn off again. Burn my limbs,' he says, 'if you ain't got a neck! And now climb up here,' he says, 'and take my neck out of the

noose. I'm as dry as a cask of split peas.'
Now you may guess that Frisco Baldo feller he
come out all over in a cold sweat. 'Git a gait
on you,' says Anty. 'I ain't going to wait up
here to please you.' So Frisco Baldo climbs
up, and a sore job he had of it getting the noose
off Anty. 'Get a gait on you,' says Anty, 'and
go easy with them clumsy hands of yours.
You'll give me a sore throat,' he says, 'the way
you're carrying on. Now don't let me fall
plop,' says Anty. 'Lower away handsomely,'
he says. 'I'll make you a weary one if you let
me fall plop,' he says. So Frisco lowers away
handsomely, and Anty comes to the ground,
with the rope off of him, only he still had his
head to one side like he'd been hanged. 'Come
here to me,' he says. So Frisco Baldo goes
over to him. And Anty he jest put one arm
round his neck and gripped him tight and cold.
'Now march,' he says; 'march me down to the
grog shop and get me a dram. None of your
six-water dollops, neither,' he says; 'I'm as
dry as a foul block,' he says. So Frisco and
Anty they go to the grog shop, and all the while
Anty's cold fingers was playing down Frisco's
neck. And when they got to der grog shop der

captains was all fell asleep. So Frisco takes
the bottle of rum and Anty laps it down like
he'd been used to it. 'Ah!' he says, 'thank
ye,' he says, 'and now down to the Mole with
ye,' he says, 'and we'll take a boat,' he says;
'I'm going to England,' he says, 'to say good-
bye to me mother.' So Frisco he come out all
over in a cold sweat, for he was feared of the
sea; but Anty's cold fingers was fiddling on his
neck, so he t'ink he better go. And when dey
come to der Mole there was a boat there — one
of these perry-acks, as they call them — and
Anty he says, 'You take the oars,' he says.
'I'll steer,' he says, 'and every time you catch
a crab,' he says, 'you'll get such a welt as
you'll remember.' So Frisco shoves her off
and rows out of the harbour, with old Anty
Bligh at the tiller, telling him to put his beef
on and to watch out he didn't catch no crabs.
And he rowed, and he rowed, and he rowed, and
every time he caught a crab — whack! he had
it over the sconce with the tiller. And der
perry-ack it went a great holy big skyoot,
ninety knots in der quarter of an hour, so they
soon sees the Bull Point Light and der Shutter
Light, and then the lights of Bristol. 'Oars,'

said Anty. 'Lie on your oars,' he says; 'we got way enough.' Then dey make her fast to a dock-side and dey goes ashore, and Anty has his arm round Frisco's neck, and 'March,' he says; 'step lively,' he says; 'for Johnny comes marching home,' he says. By and by they come to a little house with a light in the window. 'Knock at the door,' says Anty. So Frisco knocks, and in they go. There was a fire burning in the room and some candles on the table, and there, by the fire, was a very old, ugly woman in a red flannel dress, and she'd a ring in her nose and a black cutty pipe between her lips. 'Good evening, mother,' says Anty. 'I come home,' he says. But the old woman she just looks at him but never says nothing. 'It's your son Anty that's come home to you,' he says again. So she looks at him again and, 'Aren't you ashamed of yourself, Anty,' she says, 'coming home the way you are? Don't you repent your goings-on?' she says. 'Dying disgraced,' she says, 'in a foreign land, with none to lay you out.' 'Mother,' he says, 'I repent in blood,' he says. 'You'll not deny me my rights?' he says. 'Not since you repent,' she says. 'Them as repents I got no quarrel with.

You was always a bad one, Anty,' she says, ' but I hoped you'd come home in the end. Well, and now you're come,' she says. ' And I must bathe that throat of yours,' she says. ' It looks as though you been hit by something.' ' Be quick, mother,' he says; ' it's after midnight now,' he says.

"So she washed him in wine, the way you wash a corpse, and put him in a white linen shroud, with a wooden cross on his chest, and two silver pieces on his eyes, and a golden marigold between his lips. And together they carried him to the perry-ack and laid him in the stern sheets. ' Give way, young man,' she says; ' give way like glory. Pull, my heart of blood,' she says, ' or we'll have the dawn on us.' So he pulls, that Frisco Baldo does, and the perry-ack makes big southing — a degree a minute — and they comes ashore at the Mole just as the hens was settling to their second sleep. ' To the churchyard,' says the old woman; ' you take his legs.' So they carries him to the churchyard at the double. ' Get a gait on you,' says Anty. ' I feel the dawn in my bones,' he says. ' My wraith'll chase you if you ain't in time,' he says. And there was an empty grave, and they put him in it, and shovelled in the clay, and the old woman poured out a bottle on the top of it. 'It's holy water,' she says. 'It'll make his wraith rest easy.' Then she runs down to the sea's edge and gets into the perry-ack. And immediately she was hull down beyond the horizon, and the sun came up out of the sea, and the cocks cried cock-a-doodle in the henroost, and Frisco Baldo falls down into a swound. He was a changed man from that out."

"Lee fore brace," said the mate above us. "Quit your chinning there, and go forward to the rope."

X

ON GROWING OLD

THE other day I met an old sailor friend at a café. We dined together, talking of old times. He was just home, on long leave, from the Indian Marine, a service in which he is a lieutenant. At first we talked of our shipmates, and of the men we had known at sea or in foreign ports; but that kind of talk was too melancholy; we had to stop. Some had fallen from aloft, and some had fallen down the hold, and a derrick had killed one and a bursting boiler another. One had been burnt in his ship, another had been posted missing. One had been stabbed by a greaser; two or three had gone to the goldfields; one was in gaol for fraud; and one or two had taken to " crooking their little fingers " in the saloons of the Far West. He and I, we reckoned, were all that remained alive of a group of fifteen who were photographed together only eleven years ago. Before we parted, my friend remarked that I had greatly changed since our

last meeting. I had grown quite grey, he said,
and I had a drawn, old look about the eyes, and
no one (this is what grieved me) would ever
think me young again. Then we shook hands
and went our ways, wondering if we should have
yet another meeting before we died.

I left him thinking of the sadness of life and
of a man's folly in not sticking to his work.
We had been friends, I thought, intimate friends,
comrades, when we had been at sea together.
We had shared our clothes, our money, our
letters from home, our work, our ease. We had
been a proverb and a by-word to a whole ship's
company. We were going to stick to each
other, we always said, and when we were old, we
hoped, we would get a job on a lighthouse, and
smoke our pipes and read the papers together,
and perhaps write a book together, or invent a
safety pawl or a new kind of logship. We had
intended all these things. We had hoped never
to separate. We had built our lighthouse in
the air, and based it in the wash of breakers.
Then life, in its strength and strangeness, had
swept us apart; and we who had been comrades
were now a little puzzled by each other. I was
wondering how it was that he could see no

beauty in poetry. He was thinking me a little touched by time, an ancient, one grown old prematurely, a fossil, a has-been.

Then I was startled to think that he was right; to think that I was, in sooth, a has-been; that I was grown grey and bent; and that I wore an overcoat. It was shocking to me. I had done with a part of my life, with my youth, with my comrades. I should have no more comrades till I died. I should have friends, and perhaps a wife, and acquaintances to ask to dinner, and people to take a hand at cards with; but of comrades I should have no more. They were things I had done with for ever. I should go a-roving no more. I should never furl a sail again with a lot of men in oilskins. I could hum to myself the chorus —

> To *my*
> Ay,
> And we'll *furl*
> Ay
> And pay Paddy Doyle for his boots,

but I should never hear it again, as I once heard it, on the great yellow yards, among "the crowd." That line of swaying figures on the foot-rope, and the faces under the sou'-wester

brims, and the slatting canvas stiff with ice, and
the roar and the howl of the wind, and the flogging
of the gear. Well; I had done with all
that; with that and much else. I was not
among " the crowd " any more, nor could I get
back to it. Those places on the map too, those
haunting places, those places with the Spanish
names, those magical places. Oh, you names,
you beautiful names!

Then I thought that, after all, if my youth
were gone, the fine flower of it, the beauty, was
yet mine. That man, my friend, my old comrade,
what had youth been to him? It had been
a means to an end, a state of probation, the
formula that made his present. Had it any
value to him? Did it haunt him? Did it come
flooding to his mind in the night watches? Did
it say to him, " This was life, this was truth, this
was the meaning of life "? Could his soul inhabit
that past, like a king in a palace?
What, of his life, had seemed significant to
him? What, in the past, recurred to him?
Did anything? I called to mind our first voyage
together, with its long, long walks on the
deck, under the stars, over the sharp shadows
of the sails. I remembered the first whale we

saw, and the intense silvery brightness of his spout against the blue water. It had been in a dog watch, and I had been washing on the booby-hatch, and we spoke a great sailing ship an hour later. She had come to the wind about half a mile away, a noble, great ship, under all sail. I remembered her name, the *Glaucus*, and the extreme stateliness with which she dipped, and then rose, and again dipped, in a slow, swaying rhythm. I remembered the first land we made after our long sailing. We had had the morning watch, and had seen the land at dawn, a faint blue on the horizon, topped with a bright peak or two that were ruddy with sunrise. The water alongside was no longer blue, but a dark green, which was not like the seas we had sailed. As it grew lighter the mist which had lain along the land was blown away. We saw the land we had come so far to see, the land we had struggled for, the land we had talked of. It lay in a line to leeward, a grey, irregular mass, with the sun shining on it. Over us was a sky of a deep, kindly blue, patrolled with soft, white clouds, little white Pacific clouds, delicately rounded, like the clouds of the Trade

Winds. Under us was the green, tremulous, talking water, and there, towards us, came the birds of those parts, birds of the sea, flying low, dipping now and then for fish. Later, as we drew nearer, we saw the houses, the factory chimneys, the lighthouse, the gleam of a window. There were the ships in the bay, tier upon tier of them, their masts like a fence of sticks round a sand-dune. Over the quiet sea came a little tug, a little wooden tug, with her paint gone, with blisters on her smoke-stack. Slowly she came, clanging and groaning, making a knot an hour. Aboard her were the men we had come so far to see, the strangers, the men with Spanish names. In a few minutes we were to speak with them, we were to speak with strangers, the first we had met for four months. We should hear strange voices, we should see strange faces, they would have news for us. Eagerly we watched them, till the heads that had been dots upon her deck were become human. She drew up to us, clanging and groaning; she came within hail. We saw them, those strangers. A negro with a red cap; a little, pale man, smoking a cigar; a tall, brown fellow, his teeth green with coca;

and a boy in a blue shirt teasing a monkey with a stick. Those were the strangers, the men we had come to see, the men we had struggled to through the months of sailing.

That was youth, the flower of youth, the glory of it, the adventure accomplished. It had been much to me; it is much still. It had been much to my friend; it was nothing to him now. I was getting old; yet the thing came back to me, I took a part in it. The thing comes back to me; the tug, the green water, the negro with the cap, the masts of the ships at anchor. It is eternal, it is my youth, I am young in it. It is my friend who is old; it is he who has lost his youth, it has gone from him, it is dead, he has lived his vision.

But when we get to our lighthouse he will have more of such tales to tell me than I to tell him. He has seen so much. He is still seeing so much. He will have a fuller memory to turn over, and arrange, and select from. And when our pipes are smoked out, and it is time for us to go to our hammocks, it is not great poetry we shall sing together. It will be the song we sang when we were comrades, when we sailed the green seas and saw the flying fish. It will be —

ON GROWING OLD

> I dreamed a dream the other night,
> Lowlands, Lowlands, hurrah, my John;
> I dreamed a dream the other night,
> My Lowlands a-ray,

or some other song that comes with its memory of work done, its suggestion of storm and of stress and of adventure accomplished.

XI

A MEMORY

In these first frosty days, now that there is mist at dusk into which the sun's red ball drops, one can gather to the fire as soon as the lamps are lit and take the old book from the shelf, the old tune from the fiddle, and the old memory from its cupboard in the brain. Memory is a thing of rags and patches, an odd heap of gear, a bag of orts. It is a record of follies, a jumble of sketch and etching, heaped anyhow, torn, broken, blurred. One can turn it over, and see now a deck scene, with a watch at the halliards, now a woman weeping, now a carthorse tearing down a road, scattering the crowd. That is the common, haphazard, perishing memory, which is what one has to show for the privilege and glory of being man. But among these shadows, these fugitive pictures, these ghosts, there are persistent memories. Besides those angry and wretched faces, and the flaring lights, and terrible suspenses of the common records, there are

A MEMORY

others. When those pale faces cease to haunt and the sobs of the woman leave the heart unwrung for a little, then the grander memory comes flooding in, august, symbolic, like the rising of the full moon; like the coming of the tide out of the hollows of the sea. A scene, an event, some little thing, will take to itself a significant beauty. What did this mean, or this, or this? Was it that common thing, was it what we thought? It was a King passing, it was Life going by, it was life laid bare, the tick of the red heart, the face under the veil, the tune's meaning. We thought that it was this, or this; the woman's hand putting back her hair, the haze lifting from the sea. It was a revelation; it was a miracle; it was a sweeping back of Death to his place in chaos.

Now that these frosty days are on us, and the fires are lit, the memory wakens and quickens. Those recurrent images, having the strength of symbols, rise up within me, suggesting their concealed truth. That single memory, which has haunted me so long, persists. It comes to me day after day, charged with meaning, beautiful and solemn, hinting at secrets. The thing was so beautiful it could not be a chance, a mere event, finite, a thing of a day. Like all beautiful things, it is a symbol of all beauty, a hand flinging back the window, the touch bringing the grass-blade from the seed, the fire destroying Troy. All lovely things have that symbolic power, that key of release. One has but to fill the mind, and to meditate upon a lovely thing, to pass out of this world, where the best is but a shadow, to that other world, the world of beauty, " where the golden blossoms burn upon the trees for ever."

I was at sea in a sailing ship, walking up and down the lee side of the poop, keeping the time, and striking the bell at each half-hour. It was early in the morning watch, a little after four in the morning. We were in the tropics, not very far from the Doldrums, in the last of the Trades. We were sailing slowly, making perhaps some three or four knots an hour under all sail. The dawn was in the sky to leeward of us, full of wonderful colour, full of embers and fire, changing the heaven, smouldering and burning, breaking out in bloody patches, fading into faint gold, into grey, into a darkness like smoke. There was a haze on the sea, very white and light, moving and settling. Dew was dripping from the sails, from the ropes, from the eaves of the charthouse. The decks shone with dew. In the half-light of the dusk, the binnacle lamps burnt pale and strangely. There was a red patch forward, in the water and on the mist, where the sidelight burned. The men were moving to and fro on the deck below me, walking slowly in couples, one of them singing softly, others quietly talking. They had not settled down to sleep since the muster, because they were expecting the morning " coffee," then brewing in the galley. The galley funnel sent trails of sparks over to leeward, and now and then the cook passed to the ship's side to empty ashes into the sea. It was a scene common enough. The same pageant was played before me every other day, whenever I had the morning watch. There was the sunrise and the dewy decks, the sails dripping, and the men shuffling about along the deck. But on this particular day the common scenes and events were charged with meaning as though they were the initiation to a mystery, the music playing before a pageant. It may have been the mist, which made everything unreal and uncertain, especially in the twilight, with the strange glow coming through it from the dawn. I remember that a block made a soft melancholy piping noise in the mizzen rigging as though a bird had awakened upon a branch, and the noise, though common enough, made everything beautiful, just as a little touch of colour will set off a sombre picture and give a value to each tint. Then the ball of the sun came out of the sea in a mass of blood and fire, spreading streamers of gold and rose along the edges of the clouds to the mid-heaven. As he climbed from the water, and the last stars paled, the haze lifted and died. Its last shadows moved away from the sea like grey deer going to new pasture, and as they went, the look-out gave a hail of a ship being to windward of us.

When I saw her first there was a smoke of mist about her as high as her foreyard. Her topsails and flying kites had a faint glow upon them where the dawn caught them. Then the mist rolled away from her, so that we could see her hull and the glimmer of the red sidelight as it was hoisted inboard. She was rolling slightly, tracing an arc against the heaven, and as I watched her the glow upon her deepened, till every sail she wore burned rosily like an opal turned to the sun, like a fiery jewel. She was radiant, she was of an immortal beauty, that swaying, delicate clipper. Coming as she came, out of the midst into the dawn, she was like a spirit, like an intellectual presence. Her hull glowed, her rails glowed; there was colour upon the boats and tackling. She was a lofty ship (with skysails and royal staysails), and it was wonderful to watch her, blushing in the sun, swaying and curveting. She was alive with a more than mortal life. One thought that she would speak in some strange language or break out into a music which would express the sea and that great flower in the sky. She came trembling down to us, rising up high and plunging; showing the red lead below her water-line; then diving down till the smother bubbled over her hawseholes. She bowed and curveted; the light caught the skylights on the poop; she gleamed and sparkled; she shook the sea from her as she rose. There was no man aboard of us but was filled with the beauty of that ship. I think they would have cheered her had she been a little nearer to us; but, as it was, we ran up our flags in answer to her, adding our position and comparing our chronometers, then dipping our ensigns and standing away. For some minutes I watched her, as I made up the flags before putting them back in their cupboard. The old mate limped up to me, and spat and swore. "That's one of the beautiful sights of the world," he said. "That, and a cornfield, and a woman with her child. It's beauty and strength. How would you like to have one of them skysails round her neck?" I gave him some answer, and continued to watch her, till the beautiful, precise hull, with all its lovely detail, had become blurred to leeward, where the sun was now marching in triumph, the helm of a golden warrior plumed in cirrus.

XII

ON THE PALISADES

On the west side of the Hudson River there is a cliff, or crag of rock, all carved into queer shapes. It stretches along the riverside for twenty or thirty miles, as far as Tarrytown, or further, to the broad part, where the stream looks like a sea. The cliff rises up, as a rule very boldly, to the height of several hundred feet. The top of it (the Jersey shore) appears regular. It is like a well-laid wall along the river, with trees and one or two white wooden houses, instead of broken glass, at the top. This wall-appearance made the settlers call the crag "the Palisades."

Where the Palisades are grandest is just as high up as Yonkers. Hereabouts they are very stately, for they are all marshalled along a river a mile or more broad, which runs in a straight line past them, with a great tide. If you take a boat and row across to the Palisades their beauty makes you shiver. In the afternoon, when you are underneath them, the sun is shut away from you; and there you are, in the chill and the gloom, with the great cliff towering up, and the pinnacles and tall trees catching the sunlight at the top. Then it is very still there. You will see no one along that shore. A great eagle will go sailing out, or a hawk will drop and splash after a fish, but you will see no other living thing, except at the landing. There are schooners in the river, of course, but they keep to the New York shore to avoid being becalmed. You can lie there in your boat, in the slack water near the crag-foot, and hear nothing but the wind, the suck of the water, or the tinkle of a scrap of stone falling from the cliff face. It is like being in the wilds, in one of the desolate places, to lie there in a boat watching the eagles. Then you can row round to the landing, where there is a sort of beach of crumbled stone. You can go ashore there to a sort of a shack, where the jetty-keeper lives. He sells Milwaukee beer and chew'n' tobacker and other temporal verities. The ferryboat only crosses twice a day, and nobody ever crosses in her except on Sundays, and she is laid up all the winter; so that he is not overworked. When I was there the jetty-keeper was an old sailor who had been in the British navy sixty years before, and had " swallowed the anchor " in Colon. He had fought in the Mexican wars; he had been on the trail with Bigfoot Wallace; he had shaken hands with John L. Sullivan; and he had helped to bombard Fort Sumter at the beginning of the Civil War. He used to tell all sorts of yarns.

I remember that one of his yarns was about an English frigate, the *Pique*, or the *Blonde*, or the *Blanche* (or some other ship with a French name), the captain of which was an Honourable somebody with great ideas of discipline. I could never quite make out whether he had been aboard this ship, or whether he had been in port with her, or whether the whole story was hearsay. He used to give three versions of the tale. One of them began: " When I was in the King's service — it was King William was King of England then — I was a royal yardman aboard the — say the *Blonde*. She was on the South American station." Another version ran: " I was in Valparaiso one time. I come there in a brig from Port Madoc, under Captain Jenkins." The third version was less realistic. It used to begin: "There was a ship in them days called the *Blonde*. She was on the South American station. Her captain was an Honourable or else a Lord. He was a toe-the-liner, he was." The tale itself was curious, but I have not been able to prove it to be true. The one constant detail of the yarn was that the scene was Valparaiso Bay. The name of the ship is doubtful, the evidence of my friend extremely unreliable, and the date of the supposed event by no means settled. The yarn was as follows (I adopt text C as the safest) : —

"There was a ship in them days called the *Blonde*. She was on the South American station. Her captain was an Honourable or else a Lord. He was a toe-the-liner, he was. He used to polish the cap-squares; that was how he begun. Then he had all his guns and carronades kept bright. You could see your face in them. Her decks were African oak. And you must know it's not an easy job to get a African oak deck to look white. No, sir, it isn't that. Even if you sand it, it still looks a sort of a pale muddy colour. Now this Honourable Lord he was death on having his decks white. He used to work his people's irons up over them

decks. He'd work them over them decks all the
afternoon watch. And he was death on reefing
topsails. Reefing topsails in stays, that was
his lay. You never see'd that kind of play-act-
ing. He'd put his helm down and let go his
topsail halliards, and he'd have his men aloft,
and laid out, and the earrings passed, and the
three reefs took, and the men down from aloft,
and the yards hoisted, by the time it was 'let go
and haul.' It was well done, too. Them topsails had a good look along the yard, like they'd
been well lighted out, or there was a jim hickey
of a stink raised. And the last man up got
his back scratched, and the last man down got
his grog stopped. They knowed how to flog in
them days, too. But they were smart, all right.
They'd get a line-of-battle ship under all sail,
every mortal rag she had, in a minute and a
half. And they'd shift topmasts in an hour
and a half. And they'd send up topmasts and
cross topgallant yards in under five minutes.
They were smart, all right; but if you weren't,
you got it over the shoulders, man-of-war style.
Now aboard the *Blonde* they were smartened up
till they walked away from every one. And this
Honourable Lord he'd walk the quarterdeck

with his watch and all. And if it wasn't done
'on the knocker,' why, he'd have it all over
again. I tell you, aboard the *Blonde* they were
sick of the sight of him. They had that ship
all scraped and jim-dandied, and every rope
like it had been ruled, and every gun like a mirror. They were afraid of turning in at night.
They were. It's a fact. They got to hate
taking their hammocks from the nettings, there
was such a fuss made when they stowed them
in the morning.

"And while she lay at Valparaiso they were
ground for fair. They were put through it like
a circus. It was 'Shift topmasts,' or 'Down
topgallant yards,' or some gummy backache or
another all the whole day long. I guess that
Honourable Lord thought he'd took the road
with a theatre troupe. There was a Yankee
frigate in Valparaiso. He used to cross yards
against her. My hat, he used to grind them
down against that Yankee frigate. *She* wasn't
any slouch neither. No, sir; she wasn't that.
She could do her piece. But this here *Blonde*
she give her the turn-down.

"So at last all hands had had about enough
of having their old irons worked. So they

turned out one night, and they got some crows and things, and they hove every gun out of its carriage and dumped it into the bay. And they did the same with every carronade, and with every musket, and every pike, and every pistol, and every ax, and every cutlass. 'Into the bay with you,' they said. That's what they said. 'Into the bay with you. Them Chilaneans'll be glad to have you,' they said.

"So when the morning dawned they'd made a clear ship. Yes, sir; a clear ship. Not a weapon in her, but the officers' swords and the master's speaking-trumpet. There they were. Eighty ton of weapons gone through the ports. There was a gay conundrum for the Honourable Lord to crack. And what d'ye think he did?

"He called all hands, and he fell in the marines, and he read the Articles of War, and he flogged the whole ship's company. And when each man was tied up the ship's company give a cheer to make him stick it out. And when each man was being flogged the crews of all the ships in port gave three groans for the Honourable Lord. Three hollow groans. They was lying in the tiers there, you know. Moored head and stern, in with the merchant ships. And when each man was being flogged the crews all give three groans. Ugh! Yah yer! Three hollow groans. And when all hands was flogged they give three cheers. And the Yankee captain sent aboard a fishing-rod to help him get his guns up."

XIII

THE REST-HOUSE ON THE HILL

In a town it is easy to despise the visionary, for in a town there are policemen and electric lights to make difficult that fear of the dark which is the beginning of folk-lore. Out on the hills the darkness is still terrible. Among the whin and granite a man trespasses upon immortal tribes if he wanders out after the evening star has risen. In a town a man can join a folk-lore society, and attend a dinner once a year, at ten and sixpence, but out on the hills he must put milk on the doorstep on St. John's Eve and fix scraps of rag on the thorns of certain bushes. I have never seen " them " myself, but in this haunted cabin where I sit, and at the only cabins within sight, there are men and women who have seen and dealt with them. " There's many places here is gentle," says an old labourer. " There is, indeed," says his old wife. "Tell him about the time you were crossing the back-hills your lone."

"It was a great many years ago," says the old man, "and one night I had to go to see my brother. I was working at that time over at Killina, and my brother was over the hills at Clogh-na-Steuchan, a matter of eleven miles. It was nearly dark when I started, and the roads was heavy: but I was a great walker in them days, and I was got as far as where you can see them trees by about nine o'clock, or half an hour later. I was going along on the path when I saw some one in front of me. It was a gentleman-looking man, a nice, tall, gentleman-looking man, the handsomest man I ever saw, except it was yourself stepping. 'It's a fine night,' he says. 'It is, indeed,' I says. 'Where are ye going?' he says. 'I'm going to Clogh-na-Steuchan,' I says. 'You cannot,' he says. 'But I must,' I says. 'You cannot,' he says; 'you cannot go to Clogh-na-Steuchan this night.' 'Who'll stop me?' I says. 'There's them upon the hills,' he says, 'as'll stop any mortal man as tries to go this night.' 'And what'll I do?' I says. 'There's them upon the hills,' he says, 'wants no one by to see them.

REST-HOUSE ON THE HILL 125

You could stay the night at the rest-house here.' 'Where is there a rest-house here?' I says, for I knew there was none. 'You can come in my car,' he says. And then I saw he had a car with a black horse hitched to it; so I got into the car, and he drove me down a loaning. 'Now, mind yourself,' he says, 'in this rest-house. They'll offer you food, and you mustn't eat. They'll offer you drink, and you mustn't sup. They'll speak to you, and you mustn't answer. They'll give you a bed, and you mustn't sleep. And you'll come away, and you mustn't look back till you're a quarter of a mile from the door.' So then we came to the door of the house, and I got down from the car and I knocked at the door, and I was frightened at him telling me. There was an old woman came to the door with a light in her hand. 'Who are you?' she says; 'and where d'ye come from?' But I remembered what the man had said, so I didn't answer. 'Well, come in,' she said. 'Come in, dumb man,' she said. 'Come in and have a bit of supper.'

"So I went in to the door, and inside it was like a large cottage, with turf on the fire and plates on the dresser, and a few strange men sitting round on chairs, and none of them gave me the blessing of God. There was a big pot on the fire, and the woman stirred it, and every time she stirred it there came a noise out of the pot like there was a wounded man in it. So they gave out the food, but I wouldn't have any; and they were angry with me because I refused. 'They're too proud to eat with poor folk, them Carrigh boys,' said one of them. And wasn't that wonderful, that they should know where I came from, and I never seeing them before? Then one of the men brought out a bottle of whisky. And all the time he had it in his hand there was a queer kind of music coming out of it, and there was another queer kind of music running all round the dresser. It made me all cold to hear it; so I wouldn't have any of the whisky, and they were angry with me at that. 'They're temperance down at the Point in these times,' they said, and then they all laughed; and that was wonderful too, their knowing about the Point. Then the men went to a sort of bed there was, to lie down. It was a bed like the beds in a carman's rest; just one big bed for a dozen men to sleep on. There was no clothes; only just the bed, and the head part was raised instead of there being a pillow. So I lay down too, but I wouldn't go to sleep; I lay awake. And one of the men said, 'Here's a lad can't sleep,' he says; 'bring him a quilt and a pillow,' he says. So they brought me a quilt and a pillow so that I should sleep easy; but I wouldn't have them — I was feared of falling asleep, because of what the man said. So they were angry with me at that. 'These Flahertys is like cats. They sleep in the day,' they said, and then they all laughed. And wasn't that very wonderful, that they should know my name? I think it was a wonder of wonders that they should know that, and I a stranger. So then I lay awake until it was an hour before daybreak, and then I heard a cock crow, and I got up and went out of the house. And before I'd gone twenty yards there was one of them called out after me, 'Come back here; come back and have some breakfast.' But I never turned my head, because of what the man said. I just kept straight on up the loaning. And before I'd gone another hundred yards I heard one come running behind, and I knew he would try to make me look back. And he called out: 'Hey, there, Flaherty! John! You've left your pipe behind.' But I'd left my pipe at home. I was wanting it before I met with the fellow on the hill; so I just walked on fast and paid no heed to him. I just let him blather. And before I'd gone another hundred yards there was another one come running behind. 'Help, help!' he was singing out. 'The thatch is caught fire. The house'll be destroyed itself.' But I was feared of looking back, and I kept on without turning. And immediately I heard them all come hurrooing and screaming like scholars come out of a school, like young colts galloping in the dew of the day. But I never so much as turned an inch of my head; no, not so much as a hair under my hat. And when I'd got a full quarter of a mile away I looked round. And there was no house at all there; no house at all. It was nothing but just the bare hill; just the bare hill, with the stones, and the gorse growing, and no house, and no loaning, and nothing on it at all. So I walked on, giving praises to Almighty God that I was quit of them. And I got to my brother about daybreak; and he was feared I had fallen into a bog. Wasn't that wonderful, now? Wasn't that very wonderful? It was a wonder, and a wonder of wonders, that was. There was magic in it, strong magic. They're strong. They're very strong. It's not good to be saying too much about them. There's a power of queer things they do be knowing. They're knacky with it, the same as the Devil of Hell."

XIV

GENTLE PEOPLE

My friend the old labourer was "never much bothered" by the fairies. They leave folk alone, he says, if they aren't meddled with; but they have a way of stealing children from the cradle, and sometimes they steal brides from the church door, if people are so careless as to omit certain rituals which keep them at a distance. His brother, he tells me, married the beauty of the town when he was a young man. They had a little girl, who was so beautiful that all felt anxious, lest she should be spirited away by those who are ever covetous of mortal beauty, and mortal innocence. When she was a few months old the father happened to be coming home late at night, along one of the little-used "loanings" leading from the high road to his cabin. It was a fine, dark night, and he was thinking of nothing in particular, except perhaps the chances of the crops, when he heard a piping and crying as though all the fiddles and pipes in Ireland were making a music by the side of the road. There was a stamping and hurrying of feet, like a regiment charging; and there were little wild cries and little sharp songs in the air, "as though it was birds in a cornfield." He looked towards the noise, and saw, coming towards him, a company of little people in grey, all singing and dancing and playing music, and moving as fast as the following of waves in a storm. He drew to one side of the road to let them pass him, and he crossed himself vigorously till they were gone. He saw that they were carrying a little child's coffin, and that they were dancing about the coffin as they marched. They had red caps on them, and little grey coats, "all made so lovely as you'd be seeing." When he saw the coffin his heart sank low. "My child is dead," he said, and at that he fell to running to his home as fast as his legs would carry him. When he got to the door he tried to open it, but it was locked on the inside. "Let me in," he says. "For the love of God, let me in." And his wife said, "God save us. Who is that beating on the door?" And she let him in. "Is the child dead?" says he. "Is the child dead?" "The child is not dead, indeed," she says. "What ails you, anyway? The child is well enough." So he looked at the cradle, and the child was sleeping quietly. " I was feared for the child," he said; " did you not hear anything passing the door?" "I did," she said; " I heard the greatest fiddling and piping you ever heard. There was a noise outside that door like an army of pipers, like a great wind in the tree-tops; I was feared to look out." The next day they learned that it was a neighbour's child that had been taken — owing, no doubt, to the mother's neglect of one of the preventive rites.

Some fairies are solitary. The old man showed me a little holding owned by a farmer who had been helped by a lonely fairy for many years. They called him the Cluricaun, he says, and he would do all the work of the house, and most of the field work too. He would milk the goats and cows, stack the turf, feed the chickens, rub down the horse, and help to win the hay. He would mix the bread, keep the fire in, see the hearth swept, and boil all the potatoes. He had little bare feet on him, and when the roads were muddy he would leave a little track where his feet sank into the mud. One day the farmer

thought it was a shame that the Cluricaun
should go barefoot in all the mud, with the
thorns and the gorse-spikes sticking to him; so
he sewed a pair of shoes for him. They were the
neatest little shoes that ever went on a foot.
The farmer left them in the corner of the hearth
where the Cluricaun used to pass the nights.
In the morning they were gone, and the Cluricaun with them. He never came back again.
When he saw the pair of shoes left out for him
he thought that it was meant for his wages, and
that he wasn't wanted any longer. So away he
went, and they lost him; though often in the
winter mornings they would have been glad to
have heard him at the milk-pails.

Other solitary fairies are less friendly to
human beings. On one of the loneliest of these
lonely hills there is a cabin where an old woman
lives. She must be five hundred yards from her
nearest neighbour, and she has never seen a railway and never been in a boat. She has lived
so long upon the borderland of the two worlds
that she is as much at home with Them as with
men and women; but sometimes They play queer
tricks upon her. She was making her soda-bread one morning when an old pedlar-woman

came to her door asking her to buy a kettle. "I haven't the price of it," she answered. "It's only fi'pence," said the pedlar-woman. "I haven't the price of it," she answered. "You have the price of it," said the pedlar-woman. "Don't you be telling me any lie, now. You have the price of it, and twopence more than the price of it — in the eggcup on the dresser," and with that she turned away, and when the old woman looked out after her there was no sign of any pedlar there. "It was a queer thing," said the old woman, "that they should know I had sevenpence on the dresser. It was strong magic taught them. They're bothersome at whiles, but whiles they're not so bothersome. They're great ones for piping on the back hills. They make the loveliest music you ever heard. It would draw your heart out of your body."

When she was a girl they gave her a great scare. She had gone out to gather sticks for firing, and, partly in ignorance, partly in carelessness, she broke off a dead branch from one of the "fairy thorns" growing in a field. She laid her bundle of sticks upon the ground while she broke the branch into convenient lengths.

As she placed them in her bundle and prepared to carry it home a little shining golden bird alighted on the sticks, with his feathers ruffled and a song coming out of his mouth that would beat all the fiddles that ever made a tune. She was so frightened at the bird that she left her bundle on the ground and ran home. One or two other people came to take the bundle after that; but the bird was always perched upon it, and none of them would take it while the bird was there. The bundle lay on the field for nearly forty years, until the last stick of it had rotted; but while it lasted the people used to go to it on Sundays to hear the bird's song.

It is always bad to break a twig from a fairy thorn tree. Not far from here there is a great fairy tree which is very, very old and beginning to decay. It stands by the side of a frequented road. In one of the storms of last year a branch of it was broken, so that it fell across the road. It was very much in the way — indeed it stopped all wheeled traffic; but no one would presume to lay hands upon the "gentry's" wood. Men and women would go round the branch as it lay (they would not step over it), but none of them would touch it to move it to one side. At last, when the matter had become a public nuisance, the priest took it in hand, and the evil chance and the branch were thrust to one side together. It was under this tree that the musical instrument was found. "It was a musical instrument belonging to the fairies. It was like a small hoop of silver or some shining metal, and there was little bells all around it, hung on to the hoop." I tried to find out the owner of this "bell-branch," but I was told that it had disappeared soon after it was found. "They came for it one night," said the old man. "Maybe them little things had a value for it." I have heard of an English girl who left out her doll's clothes to dry upon a bush after a great doll's washing. Among the clothes were a little red woollen coat and some little socks or stockings. The old cook found these things in the early morning, and thought that they had been left by the fairies. "Amn't I lucky," she said, "to find these things left by the fairies?" When she was told that the things were doll's clothes she would not believe it. "They've got turned-back cuffs on the sleeves," she said. "There's no doll's things

GENTLE PEOPLE

has cuffs the like of that." So she kept the doll's clothes, and no doubt she felt that they brought her luck. It is easy to be lucky when one feels that the stars are on one's side.

XV

SOME IRISH FAIRIES

THERE are not many fairies in England. The English night is peopled by a grimmer folk, for whom one would never leave milk at the door nor a bunch of primroses upon the thatch. There is no appeasing these folk. They are the wraiths of bad men and witches. They live the life they lived on earth, preying darkly upon the "substance" of the spirit, as of old they preyed upon their bodies.

In Gloucestershire, at a cross-roads, there is the grave of a highwayman, with a finger-post for a headstone. He was hanged about half a mile from where he lies, and his burial was at midnight, without religious rites. This man (his name was Martin) had a favourite setter, which would not stir from his master's grave, nor take food, till he dwindled to death. The ghost of the highwayman is quiet enough; but the loving dog cannot rest. It is a charitable wraith, as in life; and though sometimes "it flounces out on you," it means no manner of harm. On a dark night, if you pass that crossing, uncertain of your road, you have only to say, "Martin's Dog, give me a light," and instantly the roads are lit by great glowing dog's eyes, bigger than the moon, to show you your road and to keep you from a natural nervousness. This dog is the only charitable "spirit" I have heard of in this country. In Ireland, on the whole, the well-meaning "spirits" are quite common; though sometimes even they play absurd and irritating tricks. Trooping fairies are generally less well-disposed than those who, like the cluricaun, or the pooka, go alone. The pooka is a pleasant creature; the cluricaun sometimes works with a family for years together. Only one fault can be found with the Irish spirits. They are arbitrary creatures moving in a fantastic world of their own. They are outside life. In England the spirits are seldom so airy. They keep pretty close to the earth. They do not live in water, or ride upon the wind. They have many of the attributes, and some of them the passions, of humanity. In Ireland they are sometimes so "detached" that they are almost out of human sympathy.

An old Irish labourer told me that once, when he was sitting by a stone fence with his father, a halfpenny leaped out on to a large flat stone and began dancing and singing. Both thought that some boy on the other side of the wall was playing them a trick; but when they looked over, there was nobody there. They knew then that "They" were at their pranks; so they watched and listened to the halfpenny with more than common interest. It danced and sang very prettily, " with a wee noise to it, like some one plucking a fiddle-string." Its dancing was partly step-dancing, leaping up and coming down in measure, like the taps of a drum; partly of that older, symbolic kind of dancing, of whirling round in a variety of circles, which, while complete in themselves, slowly described a larger circle. After making sport for half an hour the halfpenny became tired, and paused for breath. As it lay down, the father took hold of it and put it in his pocket, and carried it home. He placed it in a small wooden box upon the dresser, where it lay very still until the lamp was lit at dusk.

Then it began to sing again; but in a different note. Instead of singing like a twitched fiddle-string, it chirped like a cricket, its note getting shriller and shriller " till you would have thought it was bagpipes playing." As the note became shrill, it began to dance; and its dancing was no longer gentle, but noisy like the hammering of nails, or the grunting of oars in their crutches, or the falling of shingle when the sea is high. It did not get tired, as before. It danced and sang till it had the cottage shaking, till the neighbours came running to know what ailed them, till one would have thought the end of the world was come. All that night it danced and sang, so that they " were feared to touch it." They had no sleep at all that night; indeed they thought that the cabin would come down upon them; and glad they were when the dawn broke, and the creature, whatever it was, felt the need of a little rest. At the morning meal, before starting for work, the family debated what was best to be done. All agreed that the thing could not be thrown away; that was not to be thought of; yet they could not have such a creature in the house another night. While they were debating the point, a " poor man" came to the door, and asked for help in the name of God. The father thought that there would be a blessing, rather than ill-luck, in giving the man the halfpenny; so he gave it to him, and the beggar went his way in all happiness. But by the middle of the day, as they were working in the fields, they heard the piping and dancing coming from the cabin as before. The halfpenny had come back from the beggar man; and there it was twirling in the box again, as merry as a colt in a hay-lot. "What shall we do now?" said the father. "Maybe the priest would quiet it," said the son. "I wouldn't be bothering his reverence," said the father, "with a wee thing the like of that." "It's little bread I'll be baking, with that thing carrying on," said the mother. "You were best show it to the priest." "I will not show it to the priest," said the father. "I'll give it a strong twist over the rocks into the sea." So he went out of doors and down the little track to the beach, and there he gave the halfpenny a strong twist into the sea. And immediately it turned in the air, and flew back and struck him on the cheek, and gave three hops back on to the dresser. "There's strong magic in that," said the father. "It's a powerful magic, indeed, is in it," said the mother. "You were best burn it." "I would not be burning it for all the gold of the world," said the father. So he took hold of it again, and carried it " up the road a piece," to a fairy thorn tree, all stuck about with votive rags and ribbons. He laid it down carefully at the foot of the tree. "Lie there," he said. "There's soft lying and sweet dreams," he said, "under a tree the like of that." When he had done this, he turned to go home; but he hadn't gone the half of a perch when he heard little cries and little pattering steps behind him, and there was the halfpenny again, coming after him "in standing leps," like the devil came through Athlone. He was upset at the sight; but he put the coin in his pocket and took it back to his home. "He'll not stay under the thorn," he said. "Maybe we were wrong to take him from the fence." "Maybe it's a sup of milk he wants," said the mother; but the milk she offered was left untouched in its saucer. It was liberty, not milk, he wanted. So at last the old man and his son walked up the road to the fence and laid the halfpenny on the large flat stone. And they

had no sooner laid him down than he gave a
long leap and a whistle, and skipped away out
of that, like a salmon in the sea. They never
saw him again, though sometimes they would
hear him laughing at them from somewhere by
the side of the road.

In a village in the north of Ireland there is
a young man, who was walking home one night
after being out in a boat. He had not far to
walk; but his path took him across a field in
which a fairy thorn tree grows. It was shortly
after sunset when he entered the field, but he
did not reach his home until the morning. All
the night long he was wandering about the field,
trying to get out of it, following illusive tracks
and often falling headlong. They had bewitched him out of sheer mischief, so that he
couldn't tell which way to turn at all. Long
before the morning he was tired, but he did not
dare to sleep there, for he knew that if he fell
asleep there he would wake witless. At last,
when it grew light, they ceased from troubling,
and he was able to see the path to the fence,
with his cabin a little way beyond. He was so
weary with walking that he could do nothing
all that day.

In a field at the back of the young man's cabin there is a sousterrain, or "Dane's dwelling," a sort of underground passage, lined with stones, leading to an inner chamber. There are several of these dwellings in the district, but this one is larger than most of them and in a finer situation. It is said to contain treasure, both gold and silver; and not many years ago a man went down it and brought back a golden spoon. Others have gone down since then; "but it is likely they were angry at the spoon going," for no one has found any more treasure, owing to the magic they have put upon it. A few months back thé owner rolled a great stone across the entrance, so that his sheep should not fall down it, as they grazed over the field. The next morning the stone was rolled from the mouth; though "it was a great stone, would take three men to shift." The farmer called his men, and the stone was prised back with levers; but the next morning it was lying on its face twenty yards from the mouth of the dwelling. The farmer was not going to be beaten by either a Dane or a Druid; so he hove the stone back to its place and piled other stones against it. The next morning they were all scattered down the hill, and the dwelling lay open to the world. The farmer again rolled back the stone and put a strong curse upon it, and set men to watch there through the night. In the early morning they all fell asleep, and while they slept the stone was rolled from the door and sent spinning down the hill, through a stone fence, into the road. That angered the farmer; so he gathered all his men and poured a whole cartload of rocks down the opening, and then built a cairn on the top of it. "That'll keep you in," he said. "It's that or death," he said. The stones were too much for "Them"; they never moved one of them. The Dane's dwelling has been closed ever since.

The old man who tells me most of my stories once said that one of his greatest pleasures was to sit by the sea, listening to the music. Very sweet music comes out of the sea, he says; and he thinks "it is the salmon do be making it"; for after the salmon leave the coast the music is rarely heard. The music is soft and gentle, and rather like the old Irish harps. It is "music," not "tunes," which comes from the sea, so that it can't be mermaids; for the mermaids sing tunes, and sometimes the fishers learn the tunes and sing them at the regatta, " or wherever there is singing." The salmon music is less often heard than of old, when the rivers were watched in the spawning season; but in a good salmon year, he says, " the people come down from the hills to hear it," especially at high tides, in calm weather. " The bees sing, too," he says, " and there's a little bird on the hills sings; but there's none of them sings like the salmon, unless it was one of the Saints of God."

XVI

THE CAPE HORN CALM

OFF Cape Horn there are but two kinds of weather, neither one of them a pleasant kind. If you get the fine kind it is dead calm, without enough wind to lift the wind vane. The sea lies oily and horrible, heaving in slow, solemn swells, the colour of soup. The sky closes down upon the sea all round you, the same colour as the water. The sun never shines over those seas, though sometimes there is a red flush, in the east or in the west, to hint that somewhere, very far away, there is daylight brightening the face of things.

If you are in a ship in the Cape Horn calm you forge ahead, under all sail, a quarter of a mile an hour. The swell heaves you up and drops you, in long, slow, gradual movements, in a rhythm beautiful to mark. You roll, too, in a sort of horrible crescendo, half a dozen rolls and a lull. You can never tell when she will

THE CAPE HORN CALM

begin to roll. She will begin quite suddenly, for no apparent reason. She will go over and over with a rattling clatter of blocks and chains. Then she will swing back, groaning along the length of her, to slat the great sails and set the reef-points flogging, to a hard clack and jangle of staysail sheets. Then over she will go again, and back, and again over, rolling farther each time. At the last of her rolls there comes a clattering of tins, as the galley gear and whack pots slither across to leeward, followed by cursing seamen. The iron swing-ports bang to and fro. The straining and groaning sounds along her length. Every block aloft clacks and whines. The sea splashes up the scuppers. The sleepers curse her from their bunks for a drunken drogher. Then she lets up and stands on her dignity, and rolls no more perhaps for another quarter of an hour.

It is cold, this fine variety, for little snow squalls are always blowing by, to cover the decks with soft dry snow, and to melt upon the sails. If you go aloft you must be careful what you touch. If you touch a wire shroud, or a chain sheet, the skin comes from your hand as though a hot iron had scarred it. If you but scratch your hand aloft, in that fierce cold, the scratch will suppurate. I broke the skin of my hand once with a jagged scrap of wire in the mainrigging. The scratch festered so that I could not move my hand for a week. It was a little scratch, the eighth of an inch long. It has left its mark. The sailors used to prophesy that it would cause the loss of my arm.

On the whole we had an easy time of it in the Cape Horn calm. No work was being done about decks. Our rigging was all set up, our blocks all greased and overhauled, our chafing gear in its place, and the heavy-weather sails bent. When we came on deck we had little to do but stand by ready for a call, while the flurries of snow blew past and the ship's planking creaked. The old man was fond of mat-making. I don't know how he made the mats, whether with a " sword," in the usual way, or by a needle upon canvas. He used the coarse thread of bunting for his material. He made the boys unravel some old signal flags into little balls of thread while we were rolling in the swell. That was nearly all the work we did while the calm lasted.

THE CAPE HORN CALM

When we were down below in the half-deck, the little room twelve feet square, where the six boys lived and slept, we were almost happy. We had rigged up a bogey stove, with a chimney which kinked into elbows whenever the roll was very heavy. It did not burn very well, this bogey stove, but we contrived to cook by it. We were only allowed coke for fuel, but we always managed to steal coal enough either from the cook or from the coal-hole. It was our great delight to sit upon our chests in the dog watch, looking at the bogey, listening to the creaking chimney, watching the smoke pouring out from the chinks. In the night watches, when the sleepers lay quiet in their bunks behind the red baize curtains, one or two of us who kept the deck would creep below to put on coal. That was the golden time, the time of the night watch, to sit there in the darkness among the sleepers hearing the coals click.

One of us in each night watch made cocoa for the others. At about four bells, when the watch was half through, the cocoa-maker would slink below to put the kettle on to boil and to mix the brew in the pannikins. There is an old poet (I think it is Ben Jonson; it may be Marlowe) who asks, "Where are there greater atheists than your cooks?" I would ask, less rhythmically perhaps, "Where are there loftier thinkers than your cocoa-makers?" Ah, what profound thoughts I thought; what mute, but Miltonic, poetry I made in that dim half-deck, by the smoky bogey, in the night, in the stillness, amid the many waters. The kings were ashore in their palaces, tossing uneasily (as who would not) upon their purple pillows. Couriers were flogging spent horses along the roads of the world, bringing news of battle, of death, of pestilence. Soldiers were going into action. Prisoners were scraping shot in the chain gang. Women were weeping, and the huntsmen were up in America. Sitting there in the dim half-deck, watching the kettle boil, I saw it all. I was like Buddha under the holy branches. My mind filled with pictures like the magical water in the bowl of a wizard.

Then what a joy it was to take the cocoa tin, containing a greasy dark stuff of cocoa and condensed milk, already mixed. One put a spoonful into each pannikin and then a spoonful of soft, brown, lumpy ship's sugar. Then with a spoon, or with a sheath knife, one bruised the

THE CAPE HORN CALM

ingredients together. With what a luscious crunch they blended! How perfect was the smell of the crushed mixture! How it covered away, like the smell of incense at a Mass, the rude, worldly scents, such a tar, and stale Negro Head, and oilskins, and newly greased sea boots. Then, as one mixed, one would hear the bells struck. Ting, ting. Ting, ting. Ting. Five bells — an hour and a half before the watch would end. One would hear the old men of the sea, the old sailors, as they shambled along to and fro biting on the pipe-stems, yarning about ships that were long ago bilged on the coral. One would hear the scraps of songs, little stray verses, set to old beautiful tunes. There was one old man who had no better voice than a donkey. He was for ever walking the deck when I brewed the cocoa, singing " Rolling Home," the most popular of all sailor songs. I think I would rather have written " Rolling Home " than " Hydriotaphia." If I had written " Rolling Home " I would pass my days at sea or in West Coast nitrate ports hearkening to the roll and the roar of it as the yards go jolting up the mast or the anchor comes to the bows.

Pipe all hands to man the capstan, see your ca — bles
    run down clear,
Heave away, and with a will, boys, 'tis to old Eng-
    land's shores we steer;
And we'll sing in joyous chorus in the watches of
    the night,
For we'll sight the shores of England when the grey
    dawn brings the light.

I used to think that stanza, as the old sailor sang it in the dark watches, the most beautiful thing the tongue of man ever spoke.

While he sang, I used to take little tentative nibbles ·at the compound in the pannikins. Have you ever been an exile, reader, at sea, in pr-s-n, or somewhere, where the simple needs of life cannot possibly be gratified? If you have you will know how that sweet mush of cocoa tasted. It was like bubbling water in the desert, like fern fronds above cool springs, like the voice of the bird in the moonlight, in the green shadows, in some southern spice garden, drowsy with odours. It was like a night in June in the forest, by the babbling brook, when the moon rises, red and solemn, over the hills where the deer feed. Ah, the taste of it! the scent of it! the hidden meaning of it!

Then as I nibbled, the kettle would come to

the boil and the brew would be made. My watch-mate would come below puffing his pipe, humming his favourite tune of "The Sailor's Wives." I would fill a pannikin and carry it aft to the boy on the poop, my watch-mate stationed there, keeping the time. Round us were the waters, dark and ghostly; the crying sea-birds; the whales with their pants and spoutings. There were the masts and the great sails filling and slatting. There were the sailors lying on the deck, their pipe-bowls ruddy in the blackness. There was the murmuring and talking sea, full of mysterious menace. And the sailors' quiet talk, and the smell of tar from the sailroom, and the man at the wheel abaft all, and the lame mate limping to the binnacle — it was all beautiful, solemn, sacred, like a thing in a dream. And then the taste of the brew, when one settled down in the half-deck. The talk we had, my sleepy mate and I; talk of work and of ships, of topsails and mermaids, the old beautiful talk of youth, that needs but a listener to be brilliant.

XVII

A PORT ROYAL TWISTER

ONCE upon a time, said the Jamaican in the tavern, there was an English buccaneer who lived in a Port Royal slum. He was a poisonous great ruffian, tattooed with a gallows upon each cheek. The sun had burnt him to the colour of old brandy. He wore a pigtail that was knotted in a strip of bunting. His trousers were of faded scarlet, having been dyed in bullock's blood. He had golden earrings made of double Spanish guineas in his ears. His hat was of fine grey Lima felt, with a brim a yard across and a crown that tapered to a point. He had always a pair of pistols in his belt, a pair of oaths upon his lips, and a pair of deadly sins upon his conscience. Billy Blood was his name, but his shipmates spoke of him as Bloody Bill.

Now Billy came home from a cruise one time with a sack of Spanish gold. He landed from his ship and went to a tavern, as is the custom

A PORT ROYAL TWISTER 157

among sailors. He called for rum and a clean clay pipe. He sat down at a table, with his sack of gold before him. "You may bring more rum," he said, "whenever I bang my pot. If Cut-throat Jake and Jim the Cowboy come here," he said, "you'd best tell them where I am." By and by Jim and Jake arrived at the tavern. "Oh, happy day," they said, "which brings back Bloody Bill. Ramon," they said, "Ramon, you barrel-tilter, fetch rum — much rum — that we may welcome home our friend." So Ramon, the little tavern lad, went and tapped a new cask, and the three friends laughed very heartily when they espied his perspicacity. Then they set to serious drinking in honour of that so fortunate return.

Towards three in the morning, Billy took a bottle of brandy and poured it into a bowl. "Let us have some burnt brandy," he remarked. "Burnt brandy crowns the night," replied his comrades. "Ho! bring in a light there, Ramon." Having lit the brandy they danced solemnly about it as it burned, singing a lyric of the forecastle. Then Billy seized the flaming bowl and drained it down at a gulp. The bowl dropped from his hands and shattered

into fragments on the floor. He took a step
backwards and a step to one side, and collapsed
upon his back like a pole-axed steer. His comrades strove for a moment to revive him by
pouring rum down his throat. They then
blacked his nose with a piece of burnt cork and
rolled away home with a song.

Now, when Billy collapsed upon the floor it
seemed to him that he fell and fell and fell, as
though he were a pebble going over a precipice.
By and by he seemed to be brought up with a
round turn, though it was all black about him
— as black as so much crape. Presently he
thought he saw a sort of a gleam in the blackness, like a slug's track upon a cellar wall or a
dead crab in the caves here. Then he thought
he heard the ticking of a dropping water-clock,
like those you buy in Lima. Then he heard a
great whir of birds, like Zips, going by in a
covey, and immediately all the birds laughed,
like so many people at a pantomime. Then
there came a roar and bang, as though he had
been fired from a gun, and there he was, blinking like an owl, in a little low room, lit by many
candles, with a fire at the one end in an open
iron basket. Now, what frightened Billy Blood

was the folk who sat there, for there was a table with benches round it, and people sitting at their drink. They weren't nice people either, not in the least like you or me, for though each wore a sort of red cloak, they had the heads of snakes, and they were smoking long clay pipes, and they were laughing in a sort of hissy chuckle. And there was a great Goat-Snake sitting at the head of the table, and whenever he spoke it sent a cold dew along Billy's spine. "Come here," he said, "Billy Blood. Do you know what's going to be done with you?" "No, sir," said Billy; "if you please, sir, I'd rather not." And directly he said that the room became dark, and it seemed to Billy that he was on the loneliest island of the world — on Desolation Island, to the south of the Diego Ramirez. It was very cold. It snowed in continual little flurries. There was a snarling green sea getting up. There was night and misery rolling in from the south and west. Oh, a bitter place it seemed — a bitter place. Then there came a gull flying past, blowing in the wind like a scrap of dirty paper. "Wheu, wheu, wheu," it cried. "Billy Blood, my son; Billy Blood, my son; wheu, wheu, wheu, and so you are here." And Billy knew the voice to be the voice of old Captain Morgan, his old captain. And immediately he felt that he too was changing to a gull; he felt that his feet were webbing and his nose growing into spoon shape. Then there came a great cackling and crying, and thither came a swarm of Cape pigeons. "Wheu, wheu," they cried, "here's old Billy Blood, old Bloody Bill, old brandy-bows." And Billy knew them to be his old shipmates, for one by one he recognized them. There was Ned that they left behind on the Chagres; there was Joe that was shot at Panama; there was Jack that got the fever at St. Mary; there were Bill and Dick that the Spaniards hung, and Jimmy that was drowned in the surf. And he felt that his skin was coming out in spots, in black and white mottles like the pigeons. Then there came a busy multitude of penguins, swimming on the waves and slapping at the water with their flappers. They laughed and mewed as they swam, and pecked at anything they saw. And Bill knew them to be the old buccaneers of the past, the men who had sailed with Drake, the men of Algiers and Thelemark — all the old raiders who had died in their shirts since water drowned. And he felt that his arms were shrinking into flappers, that his chest was getting scaly, and that his blood was three-parts oil, like a Valparaiso salad. "Let me out of this!" he screamed; "let me out of this!" And immediately he was back in the little room, with the red-cloaked snakes still smoking at the table and laughing in a sort of hissy chuckle.

"Well, Billy Blood," said the fat black Goat-Snake, "now you know what's going to be done to you." "Oh, sir," said Billy, "please, sir, not. Not that, sir; not a bird, not a gulley that the reefers catch with pork fat. Anything but that, sir," he said. "Why not?" said the Goat-Snake; "why shouldn't you be a gulley? Haven't you lied and robbed and drunk and killed till your blood is three-parts rum and your soul a thick black blot of guilt? Why shouldn't you be a gulley like your precious comrades?" Billy didn't find it easy to make an answer. "Well," said the Goat-Snake, "answer me. Why shouldn't you be a gulley? Did you ever do a single good act — one single good act — since you came to be a grown-up man?" So Billy thought for a long time. Then he said, "Please, sir, I gave a blind beggar a quoit of gold that time I was ashore in Honduras." "A lot of good that'll do to you," said the Goat-Snake. "Weren't you drunk at the time?" "Not exactly drunk, sir," said Billy, "not drunk exactly. That wasn't it. Only just merry or so." "And didn't you do it by mistake?" said the Goat-Snake. "Didn't you intend to give him the little brass plate you'd stolen from the medicine chest?" "I did, sir," said Billy; "it's true. Only I was the poorer for it. It was a good deed that way." "A gulley you must be," said the Goat-Snake. "I never heard a paltrier excuse." "Please, sir," said Billy, "there was a good deed I did when I was a lad at school." "Any port in a storm," said the Goat-Snake. "What was that?" "Sir," said Billy, "one time they tried to get me to come and rob an orchard. 'No,' I said. 'It's a widow's orchard. I will not rob a widow's orchard with any man.' Wasn't that a good deed I'd like to know?" "A lot of good that'll do to you," said the Goat-Snake. "Didn't you pinch the boys' cakes as soon as they were gone to get the apples? Wasn't that why you refused to go — so that you might rob their dinner baskets?" "You're so hard on a feller," said Billy; "you don't give one half a chance." "A gulley you must be," said the Goat-Snake. "I can't think how you were taught. I never met such a man." "There was a good deed I did, sir; really there was, sir," said Billy, "when I was a little babe in shorts." "Better crust than supperless," said the Goat-Snake. "But I must say you run it rather fine. What was that, I wonder?" "Sir," said Billy, "one time when I was teething I kept from yelling in the night, so that my poor mother got a little sleep." "I dare say they'd given you a sleeping draught," said the Goat-Snake. "But we'll let it go at that. You shall not be a gulley unless you come here again. But you mind your eye, my son. I'm not a jesting person."

And Billy woke up with a screech on the tavern floor where he had fallen, and he swore off rum from that day. He lived to be church-warden down to Dartmouth, and was actually buried in the nave.

XVIII

IN A FO'C'SLE

ASHORE, in the towns, men find it easy to amuse themselves, for there is amusement, or at least a satisfaction, in being with a number of one's fellows. No man need suffer much from introspection while opinions, ideals, and a sight of the most living of modern arts may be purchased for a few copper coins. But at sea the individual must make his own amusement or become a victim of that brooding melancholy from which so many sailors suffer. A sailing ship has always reminded me of the Middle Ages, for on board a sailing ship one meets with the last traces of the mediaeval temper. One sees in a forecastle or in a half-deck the creation of arts to fill the emptiness of life. There is no newspaper, no beer, and no music-hall when once the ship is out of soundings, so that we find sailors at sea acting precisely as the people of the Middle Ages acted, and as the country-folk of quiet districts act today. In the dog watches (or at least the second dog watch), when the day's work about decks is over, and the night watch is not yet set, the sailors beguile the time just as the old folk beguiled it in the past, in the days when wandering minstrels found a welcome in every tavern. I have seen the most of a ship's company sitting as still as statues listening to a yarn about a ghost, and I remember a young seaman getting " a bloody coxcomb " for rising from his place while a song was being sung. On one eventful passage I remember how a sailor was " sent to Coventry " for the whole homeward voyage because he would not subscribe to the joint purchase of an accordion, a musical instrument on which one of the men performed. The crew clubbed together to buy the musician his instrument, so that, like " Arion on the dolphin's back," he might play to them when work was done. One man refused to subscribe, and his refusal was visited upon him by the displeasure of all hands. I remember the man wandering about like a sort of Ishmael during the night watches, finding no one to talk with, no one to beg a chew from, and no one to lie beside in the pleasant trade winds when we slept our watches through.

Some of the yarns spun by the fo'c'sle hands are scarcely suited to quotation, and I have heard songs sung by an entire crew in chorus such as no compositor could set without danger to his morals. These yarns and songs are more common now among sailors than some forty years ago, when passages were longer and sailors more of a race apart. They raise a laugh always, but they are always less popular than the old stories, which are more purely folktales. Of these the most popular are those which tell of sailors who get the better of the mate, or " the old man," or the landsman, or the Devil. Fanciful and beautiful stories were common enough at one time, though now one must search hard enough to find them. The songs have also deteriorated. The music-hall has sent its lyrics afloat, and beautiful old songs like " Spanish Ladies," " Bunclody," and " The tide is flowing " are now seldom heard. It is, however, something that the art is reverenced even in its decadence. A good singer, a clever story-teller, a nimble dancer, or a musician is always looked upon with reverence. I remember an old sailor who refused to criticize the faulty seamanship of a mate on the ground that "he sings pretty good," as though any touch of art were sufficient to cover all shortcomings. To the simple mind the "gifted" man is one to praise or to dread. It is dangerous to speak ill of such a one. "They have ways of hearing things," as an old Irish fisherman once remarked to a friend of mine.

One winter night, off the Horn (I was aboard a sailing ship at that time), a green sea came flooding over the deck-house where I lived, smashing the skylight, and leaving two or three feet of water to wash the chests about. It broke the little "bogey" stove at which we were accustomed to boil cocoa after our tricks at the wheel and look-out. I therefore took my cocoa-tin and pothook to the fo'c'sle, where I knew I should find a fire and a welcome. The watch was just come below when I got there, and the space was filled with sailors who were busy taking off their oilskins and wringing the water from their shirts. They gave me leave to use their stove, and I set to work to make my brew, noting how warm, dry, and comfortable the fo'c'sle was, compared to the filthy kennel, knee-deep in water, from which I had come. As I watched my pot, the sailors lit their pipes, hung their wet gear to dry, and fell to sleep or to yarning, as the fancy took them. "There was a sailor once," said one old man, "and I think he wasn't much use at it anyway. By dad I don't think it. And he went to sea one time in one of them old tea-clippers, the Thames to Canton River; the *Nancy Strang* her name was. So when they gets to setting the watch the first night after leaving the Downs, the mate he comes to this feller. 'What are *you* doing?' he says. 'What's *your* name?' 'My name's Jack,' he says. 'You don't mean it?' says the mate. 'Well, Jack,' he says, 'just nip aloft there with a can of slush and grease the main royal mast; the skysail parrel don't work easy.' So Jack he greases down the royal mast, and it took him the best part of an hour, and down he come. 'I greased the royal mast,' he says. 'Oh, have you, Jack?' says the mate. 'Well, Jack,' he says, 'just nip up and overhaul them fore-skysail buntlines.' So he do that too, and down he come. 'I overhauled them buntlines,' he says. 'Have you, Jack?' says the mate. 'Why, then, you'll want a job, Jack,' he says; 'just nip aloft again and see if the main topgallant staysail cliphooks is moused.' So he do that too. Well, all that voyage it was 'Jack, just nip aloft and see what's fouling the weather main skysail brace-block'; or 'Jack, shin up that skysail pole and clear the truck halliards'; or 'Jack, aft with you with a scraper and scrape the end of the gaff.' Every nasty little worriting job they give to him. It was Jack this, and Jack that, and Jack do the other thing, till he was fairly twisted with it, the same as Barney's bull. So when they come to Canton River he was all wore to skin and bone. 'Jump in the boat there, Jack,' they says, 'and clean her out ready for the old man to go ashore.' 'I will, indeed,' he says, 'when my mother's cows come home,' he says. And he give a run and jump, and over the side he goes, and into Canton River, and up the bank into the town. 'I'll swallow the anchor of that there hooker,' he says. 'I ain't going to be wore to skin and bone,' he says; 'having my old iron worked up,' he says. 'Jack this, and Jack that, and Jack lay aft till I ground you into bath-brick. Enough of that,' he says. So he lays low among all them yellow chows, and he watches the *Nancy Strang* as she sails for the Thames. 'A good riddance, you hungry, cruel, sailor's misery,' he says. And he goes and ships in a Yankee packet bound for the Mersey. Well, the first night out the second mate comes to him. 'What's *your* name?' he says. Well, he'd had enough of Christian names on the trip out, that fellow had. So he lets on he's a stammerer. So he says, 'M M M M M M M,' like he couldn't speak straight. '*What* name?' says the second mate. 'M M M M M,' he says. 'O snakes!' says the second mate, 'be darned if we haven't got a dummy aboard. O, set down,' he says. 'Go and take a set down. You can give it me in writing in the morning. Here you there, Bill,' he says. 'Up to the main skysail there and unreeve the truck halliards.' So Jack he lies low all the run home, and not a single stroke did he get called on for, and in a Yankee ship at that."

XIX

THE BOTTOM OF THE WELL

"ONCE upon a time there was a sailor named Bill. He was a seaman, and a hard case. We sailed together in the *Aladdin* barque. She was burnt off Valparaiso a year or two later. Her old man was a son of a gun for style. You should have seen him carry cloth. When Bill was a young man he got a lot of folly — reading them novels. They're a dandy set, them writer fellers. Well, Bill he read them till he got all tied in a knot with it. He got so as he couldn't tell the truth. That's straight. He couldn't call the kettle black. I never heard such lies as he told.

"He was ashore one time, on the beach. That was at Tocopilla. Was you ever at Tocopilla? No? Well, it's the last place made. It wasn't never finished. It's an open road, Tocopilla is, and when it blows a norther you slip and skip. I was there once, and a norther come, and we was three weeks at sea. Well,

Bill was there, on the beach, doing lancher's graft — eight, nine, ten and a tally — tanning his back with nitrate. That's a great graft; two hours' work a day, and a roaring surf twice a week, so as you can't go out.

"So one time Bill was sleeping in his lanch, and he woke up sudden, and he see a little man, all blue and gold like an Admiral. He was sitting in the stern of the lanch — and there was all butterflies round him, great green and blue butterflies, all shining in the sun. So the little man looks at Bill. 'Bill, can you spin a yarn?' he says. 'I can, sir,' says Bill. 'Could you spin two, Bill?' 'I could, sir,' he says. 'Could you spin three, Bill?' says the old man again. 'Yes, sir,' says Bill. 'With what I've read, I could spin three.' 'Good-oh,' says the little man. 'Hi. Runkum. Twit.' Them was magic.

"Now, so soon as them magic words was spoken the butterflies seized the bow-painter. O, thousands of them there were, great green and blue fellers, all shining. And they flapped their wings till they sparkled, giving that hooker a tow. And she forged ahead through the sea — going steady west — and the dolphins come past, all fiery, and the flying fish come past, all bright, and the wind blows kind, and never any sprays come aboard.

"So at last they come to an island, where there was golden flowers on the trees, and a palace of marble, with a Union Jack on the chimney. So they run alongside, and the butterflies goes to the flowers, and the little man takes Bill to the palace.

"So when they come to the palace there was nothing but books, written by them novel fellers. The place was stowed with them, like a ship with dunnage. Heaps and heaps of them, new and old, big and little, Bible books and Deadwood Dickeys. You never saw such a gash of books. And all along the books there was a sort of row of cells, like in Liverpool Jail, and voices coming out of them, like in Liverpool Jail on Sunday. 'What's in them cells?' says Bill. 'Just writer fellers,' says the little man. 'Now, mind, Bill,' he says, 'you got to spin yarns to the King. Don't you go telling any lies, now. None of your Cape Horn Gospels.'

"And with that he shoves Bill through a door, and there he was, in a great big room as big as a church. It was all covered with books

— all sorts of books — and at the end of it was a King on a throne, with a sort of soldiers, with axes, standing guard by him. He was a weary-looking man, the King was. Round his throne was all books, written by them novel fellers. They're a gummy lot, them fellers. The King had been reading of them.

"So he sees Bill, and he speaks in a sort of a groan. 'I've been looking for truth,' he says; 'looking for truth in all these books, in all these stories. There's not a rat of truth in one of them. Not a solid rat, there isn't. And some of them I've got, and some of them I've not got, but I've got the biggest liars of them. They're under lock and key, they are. But I've got no truth. Not a rat of truth have I got. And I've read all these, as you see.'

"So Bill he just bows.

"'Now, Bill,' says the King, 'tell us them tales of yours. I'm sick for a true word, and that's the plain fact. Heave and she goes, now.'

"So Bill he pitches him a song and dance. 'Once upon a time,' he says, 'I was in command of the *Carrowdore* clipper. And I was bound through the Pal-am-jen-bang Straits, between

Java and Oa-moru. And you may take it from him who discovered them, them Straits is a caution. They're as narrow as Sunday Lane, and as full of rocks as a barrow is of peanuts. And I went through on a spring tide, with breakers roaring like a lot of psalm-singers. And the rocks were all close aboard. And a mermaid sat on each rock, with golden hair falling over her. And the mermaids were all playing ball with drowned men's skulls. It was tough, and I didn't like the looks of it, but "Starboard," I says. "Check in your head brace, Mr. Mate," I says. "Heave now," I says. "Heave and break your hearts." And she ran through, like a calf being chevied by a boys' school, without so much as starting a yarn.'

"And the King looks at his Prime Minister, and the Prime Minister smiles and nods his head. 'By James, Bill,' says the King, ' you've got the root of the matter in you. It rings true in every word. Now your second tale. At *once*.' So Bill he hands out another song and dance. 'Once upon a time,' he says, ' I was in command of the *Euryalus*, forty-gun ship, and I was cruising off of Cape Tiburon, suppressing them Spanish privateers. And we come across a raft with old Father Neptune on it. He was being towed by a lot of porpoise, and he was dead-oh. And the porpoise was eating shrimps while he slept. So we slip a bowline over him and hoist him on deck, and I give him dinner when he wakes. So I fill him to the chin with Navy rum, and then I pump him. "Where's them Spanish privateers?" I says. And he tells me. So then I let her go off, and I put him aboard his raft again. And I make a general average of the Spaniards, and the Queen of England made me a Knight that very next Christmas.'

"And the King looks at his Prime Minister, and the Prime Minister laughs, and they shake hands together, like in the theatre —' Ha, me brother!' Just like that. And the King turns to Bill. 'At last,' he says, 'out of the mouth of a simple person have I heard the truth — the real truth. Oh, your third story. At *once!*' So Bill he just shoves ahead and hands them out another, like they give buns at a school treat.

" 'Once upon a time,' he says, ' I was wrecked

THE BOTTOM OF THE WELL 177

on the South Pole — ran bang into it one windy night. I carried away so many splinters from it that we used it for firewood all the time we were on the raft. We were ninety-nine days drifting, and nothing to eat all that while except just whales and that — and one or two flying fish.'

"'One or two *what?*' said the King.

"'Flying fish,' says Bill; 'ordinary flying fish.'

"'Flying fish?' says the King. 'Flying fish, did you say?'

"'Yes; flying fish, of course,' says Bill. 'D'you mean to say you're a King and never heard of flying fish?'

"And the King he wept like a child. 'I thought you were bringing me the truth,' he says. 'The truth I have always longed for. And you lie about fish flying like a Portuguese pilot. Here!' he says to the guard. 'Remove this person. No, don't kill him. He is not fit to die. Turn him adrift in his boat, with some bread and water. Begone, you and your flying fish! You're the foulest liar I've ever come across!'

"So Bill he was put into his boat and turned adrift, and he mighty near got drowned. And never a lie has he ever told since then. He was that changed by the sight of that old King."

XX

BEING ASHORE

In the nights, in the winter nights, in the nights of storm when the wind howls, it is then that I feel the sweet of it. Aha, I say, you howling catamount, I say, you may blow, wind, and crack your cheeks, for all I care. Then I listen to the noise of the elm trees and to the creak in the old floorings, and, aha, I say, you whining rantipoles, you may crack and you may creak, but here I shall lie till daylight.

There is a solid comfort in a roaring storm ashore here. But on a calm day, when it is raining, when it is muddy underfoot, when the world is the colour of a drowned rat, one calls to mind more boisterous days, the days of effort and adventure; and wasn't I a fool, I say, to come ashore to a life like this life. And I was surely daft, I keep saying, to think the sea as bad as I always thought it. And if I were in a ship now, I say, I wouldn't be doing what I'm trying to do. And, ah! I say, if I'd but stuck to the sea I'd have been a third in the Cunard, or perhaps a second in a P.S.N. coaster. I wouldn't be hunched at a desk, I say, but I'd be up on a bridge — up on a bridge with a helmsman, feeling her do her fifteen knots.

It is at such times that I remember the good days, the exciting days, the days of vehement and spirited living. One day stands out, above nearly all my days, as a day of joy.

We were at sea off the River Plate, running south like a stag. The wind had been slowly freshening for twenty-four hours, and for one whole day we had whitened the sea like a battleship. Our run for the day had been 271 knots, which we thought a wonderful run, though it has, of course, been exceeded by many ships. For this ship it was an exceptional run. The wind was on the quarter, her best point of sailing, and there was enough wind for a glutton. Our captain had the reputation of being a " cracker-on," and on this one occasion he drove her till she groaned. For that one wonderful day we staggered and swooped, and bounded in wild leaps, and burrowed down and shivered, and anon rose up shaking. The wind roared up aloft and boomed in the shrouds, and the

sails bellied out as stiff as iron. We tore
through the sea in great jumps — there is no
other word for it. She seemed to leap clear from
one green roaring ridge to come smashing down
upon the next. I have been in a fast steamer
— a very fast turbine steamer — doing more
than twenty knots, but she gave me no sense of
great speed. In this old sailing ship the joy of
the hurry was such that we laughed and cried
aloud. The noise of the wind booming, and the
clack, clack, clack of the sheet-blocks, and the
ridged seas roaring past us, and the groaning
and whining of every block and plank, were like
tunes for a dance. We seemed to be tearing
through it at ninety miles an hour. Our wake
whitened and broadened, and rushed away aft in
a creamy fury. We were running here, and
hurrying there, taking a small pull of this, and
getting another inch of that, till we were weary.
But as we hauled we sang and shouted. We
were possessed of the spirits of the wind.
We could have danced and killed each other.
We were in an ecstasy. We were possessed.
We half believed that the ship would leap from
the waters and hurl herself into the heavens,
like a winged god. Over her bows came the

sprays in showers of sparkles. Her foresail was wet to the yard. Her scuppers were brooks. Her swing-ports spouted like cataracts. Recollect, too, that it was a day to make your heart glad. It was a clear day, a sunny day, a day of brightness and splendour. The sun was glorious in the sky. The sky was of a blue unspeakable. We were tearing along across a splendour of sea that made you sing. Far as one could see there was the water shining and shaking. Blue it was, and green it was, and of a dazzling brilliance in the sun. It rose up in hills and in ridges. It smashed into a foam and roared. It towered up again and toppled. It mounted and shook in a rhythm, in a tune, in a music. One could have flung one's body to it as a sacrifice. One longed to be in it, to be a part of it, to be beaten and banged by it. It was a wonder and a glory and a terror. It was a triumph, it was royal, to see that beauty.

And later, after a day of it, as we sat below, we felt our mad ship taking yet wilder leaps, bounding over yet more boisterous hollows, and shivering and exulting in every inch of her. She seemed filled with a fiery, unquiet life. She seemed inhuman, glorious, spiritual. One forgot that she was man's work. We forgot that we were men. She was alive, immortal, furious. We were her minions and servants. We were the star-dust whirled in the train of the comet. We banged our plates with the joy we had in her. We sang and shouted, and called her the glory of the seas.

There is an end to human glory. "Greatness a period hath, no sta-ti-on." The end to our glory came when, as we sat at dinner, the door swung back from its hooks and a mate in oilskins bade us come on deck "without stopping for our clothes." It was time. She was carrying no longer; she was dragging. To windward the sea was blotted in a squall. The line of the horizon was masked in a grey film. The glory of the sea had given place to greyness and grimness. Her beauty had become savage. The music of the wind had changed to a howl as of hounds.

And then we began to "take it off her," to snug her down, to check her in her stride. We went to the clewlines and clewed the royals up. Then it was, "Up there, you boys, and make the royals fast." My royal was the mizzen-royal, a rag of a sail among the clouds, a great grey rag, which was leaping and slatting a hundred and sixty feet above me. The wind beat me down against the shrouds, it banged me and beat me, and blew the tears from my eyes. It seemed to lift me up the futtocks into the top, and up the topmast rigging to the cross-trees. In the cross-trees I learned what wind was.

It came roaring past with a fervour and a fury which struck me breathless. I could only look aloft to the yard I was bound for and heave my panting body up the rigging. And there was the mizzen-royal. There was the sail I had come to furl. And a wonder of a sight it was. It was blowing and bellying in the wind, and leaping around " like a drunken colt," and flying over the yard, and thrashing and flogging. It was roaring like a bull with its slatting and thrashing. The royal mast was bending to the strain of it. To my eyes it was buckling like a piece of whalebone. I lay out on the yard, and the sail hit me in the face and knocked my cap away. It beat me and banged me, and blew from my hands. The wind pinned me flat against the yard, and seemed to be blowing all my clothes to shreds. I felt like a king, like an emperor. I shouted aloud with the joy of that "rastle" with the sail. Forward of me was the main mast, with another lad, fighting another royal; and beyond him was yet another, whose sail seemed tied in knots. Below me was the ship, a leaping mad thing, with little silly figures, all heads and shoulders, pulling silly strings along the deck. There was the sea, sheer under me, and it looked grey and grim, and streaked with the white of our smother.

Then, with a lashing swish, the rain-squall caught us. It beat down the sea. It blotted out the view. I could see nothing more but grey, driving rain, grey spouts of rain, grey clouds which burst rain, grey heavens which opened and poured rain. Cold rain. Icy-cold rain. Rain which drove the dye out of my shirt till I left blue tracks where I walked. For the next two hours I was clewing up, and furling, and snugging her down. By nightfall we were under our three lower topsails and a reefed forecourse. The next day we were hove-to under a weather cloth.

There are varieties of happiness; and, to most of us, that variety called excitement is the most attractive. On a grey day such as this, with the grass rotting in the mud, the image and memory of that variety are a joy to the heart. They are a joy for this, if for no other reason. They teach us that a little thing, a very little thing, a capful of wind even, is enough to make us exult in, and be proud of, our parts in the pageant of life.

XXI

ONE SUNDAY

TEN years ago I was "in the half-deck" of a four-masted barque. We were lying in Cardiff, loading patent fuel for the West Coast. There were six of us "in the half-deck." Saving the cook, the steward, the mate, and the old man, we were the only folk aboard. In the daytime on weekdays we bent sails, or hoisted stores aboard, or shifted topsail sheets. In the evenings we went ashore to flaunt our brass buttons in St. Mary Street and to eat sweetstuff in the bun-shops. Two of us used to drink "rum-hot" in a little public-house near the docks. One of us made love to a waitress. We all smoked pipes and cocked our caps at an angle. One of us came aboard drunk one night, in a pretty pickle, having fallen into the dock. Another of our number got kicked out of a music-hall. Youth has strange ways and strange pleasures.

On Sundays we did no work after we had

hoisted the house-flag and the red ensign. We were free to go ashore for the day, leaving one of our number aboard to act as boatman. The "old man" always told us to go to church. Sometimes he asked us for the parson's text when we came aboard again. One of the six, who had been carefully brought up, used to answer for the rest. I think he made up the texts on the spur of the moment. He is dead now, poor fellow. He was a good shipmate.

One Sunday I went ashore with the rest to spend the day in the park, playing cricket with a stick and a tennis ball. In the afternoon we went to a little teashop not far from sailor-town, a place we patronized. It was up a flight of stairs. It was a long room, with oilcloth on the floor and marble-top tables and wicker chairs and a piano. There was a framed text on the piano-top. It was all scrawled over on the unprinted part with messages to Kitty, a tall Welshwoman with but one eye, who acted as waitress. The wall was all scrawled over, too, with pencilled texts, proverbs, maxims, scraps of verses.

On this particular Sunday, when I entered, there were half a dozen other apprentices already seated at their teas. They were all West Coast apprentices; that is, they had been one or two voyages to Chili and Peru in "West Coast barques" engaged in the carriage of nitrates. They were not a very choice lot, as apprentices go, but they knew the West Coast, which we did not, and one of them, a lad named Parsons, was popular among us. He had a singularly sweet tenor voice. He is dead now, too. His ship was burned off Antofagasta. The boat he was in never came to port.

After we had finished our teas we sat about in the teashop, smoking. One of the third-voyagers — he belonged to a little barque called the *Cowley* — was chaffing Kitty and asking her to marry him. The others were yarning, and holding a Dover Court. One of them was reciting the story of William and Mabel. Another was singing a song popular at sea. Its chorus ends, "Love is a charming young boy." It is a very pretty song with a jolly tune. Another was singing "The Sailor's Wives," a terrible ballad, with a tune which is like a gale of wind.

Presently a wild-looking lad whom his mates called Jimmy, got up from his chair and went to the piano. He began to play a dance tune to which I had often danced in the days long before. He played it with a deal of spirit, and he was a good player, and the tune moved him. Coming as it did (on the top of all that silly chatter), with its memories of dead nights, and lit rooms, and pretty women, it fairly ripped the heart out of me. It stirred every reefer in the room. You could see them stirred by it, though one or two of them laughed, and swore at the player for a dancing-master. After he had finished his tune Jimmy came over to me. I thanked him for his music, and complimented him upon his playing. "Ah," he said, "you're a first-voyager?" "Yes," I said. "Then you're like a young bear," he said, "with all your sorrows to come." I replied with the sea-proverb about going to sea for pleasure. "Where are you bound?" he asked. "Junin, for orders," I answered. "I was in Junin my first voyage," he said. "My hat! I was in Junin. I was very near being there still." "Were you sick?" I asked. "I was," he said shortly. "I was that.

"Ah," he went on bitterly, "you're going to sea your first voyage. You don't know what it is. I tell you, I was sick in Junin. I lay in my bunk, with the curtain drawn, and the surf roaring all the time. It never let up, that surf. All the time I was ill it was going on. One long, long roar. I used to lie and pinch myself. I could have screamed out to hear that surf always going. And then there was a damned patch of sunlight on the deck. It almost drove me mad. She rolled of course, for she was pretty near light. And that patch kept sliding back and to, back and to, back and to. I would see nothing but that patch all day. It was always yellow, and sliding, and full of dust. You don't know what it is to be sick at sea.

" Shall I tell you what it was made me well? I was lying there in my bunk, and there was a crack ship, one of Farley Brothers'— the *Ramadan* her name was. She was homeward bound. She was next but one to us in the tier. You don't know about the West Coast? No? Well, when a ship's homeward bound the crowd cheer — cheer every ship in the port; three cheers for the *Hardy-Nute*, three cheers for the *Cornwallis*, and the ship cheered answers back one cheer. And when a ship sails all the ships in port cheer her — three cheers for the *Rama-*

dan — and she answers back one cheer. One ship at a time, of course. And every ship in port sends a boat aboard her with a couple of hands to help her get her anchor. Well, the *Ramadan* was sailing, and I was lying in my bunk as sick as a cat. And there they were cheering 'Three cheers for the *Ramadan*.' And then the one cheer back. 'Hip, hip, hip, hooray.' I tell you it did me good.

"And there I was listening to them, and I thought of how prime they must be feeling to be going home, out of that God-forgotten sand-hill. And I thought of how good the cheers must have felt, coming across the water. And I thought of them being sleepy in the night watch, the first night out, after having 'all-night-in' so long. And then I thought of how they would be loosing sail soon. You don't know what it was to me.

"And then I heard them at the capstan, heaving in. You know how it is at the capstan? The bass voices seems to get all on one bar, and the tenor voices all on another, and the other voices each to a bar. You hear them one by one as they heave round. Did you never notice it? They were singing 'Amsterdam.' It's the only chanty worth a twopenny. It broke me up not to be heaving round too.

"And when they come to get under sail, setting the fore-topsail, and I heard them beginning ' There's a dandy clipper coming down the river,' I lit out a scritch, and I out of my bunk to bear a hand on the rope. I was as weak as water, and I lay where I fell. I was near hand being a goner. The first words I said was ' Blow, bullies, blow.' It was that chanty cured me. I got well after that."

He turned again to the piano and thumped out a thundering sea chorus. The assembled reefers paid their shot and sallied out singing into the windy streets, where the lamps were being lit. As we went we shouted the song of the sea: —

> A-roving,
> A-roving,
> Since roving's been my ru-i-n,
> I'll go no more a ro-o-ving
> With you, fair maid.

XXII

A RAINES LAW ARREST

WHEN I was working in a New York saloon I saw something of the city police. I was there shortly after the Lexow Commission, at a time when the city was groaning beneath the yoke of an unaccustomed purity. The old, happy, sinful days, when a man might do as he pleased as long as he kept the police squared, were over. Roosevelt had reformed the force and made it fairly efficient, so that saloon-keepers, who had once kept open "all day long and every day," were compelled to close on Sundays, in compliance with the Raines Law. The saloon in which I worked had been accustomed to serve drinks on Sunday ever since its opening. When the Raines Law came into operation it continued its ancient custom, with the result that the police entered one Sunday morning and " pulled the joint"— that is, they arrested and fined the proprietor. Shortly after the raid I became a tender in this saloon, and had a good oppor-

A RAINES LAW ARREST 195

tunity of noting how a law might be evaded. On Sunday mornings, at about eight o'clock, the bar was carefully darkened, so that no one could view the interior from without. A vast number of beer bottles was brought up from the cellars. The ice-boxes were packed with as much ice as they would hold. A dumb cash register was produced, in order that no one in the street might hear the ringing of a bell as the bar-tender stored the cash. The main door was then curtained off and barricaded. A side door which opened on to a porch, which opened, through a second door, on to the street, was then " put upon the chain " with a trusty guard beside it. The porch door, opening on the street, was locked, and Johnna, the Italian lunchman, was placed in charge of it. It had a little square glass in the upper panel, like the slit in a conning-tower. Johnna had orders to look through this glass at those who knocked before admitting them. If he knew them he was to admit them. If he did not know them he was to ask them angrily, through the keyhole, " What-a you want? No get-a trinka here," and to pay no further attention to them. As soon as the customer had passed within the second door, into the bar, he was served with his heart's desire, in the semi-darkness; but the bottles were removed from sight directly the glass was filled, lest a " cop " should enter and find " drink exposed for sale " within the meaning of the Act.

It was a curious sight, that silent bar, with its nervous ministrants filling glasses for the greatly venturous. From behind the bar I could see Johnna sitting in the porch in his black Sunday clothes, with a cigar between his lips and an Italian paper on his knees. Sometimes he would grin across at me as I hulled strawberries or sliced pineapples for cocktails. He would open his mouth and beckon to me; and then, if the boss were not looking, I would fling a berry or a scrap of pine to him. He used to catch them in his mouth with wonderful dexterity, much as a terrier would catch flies. This, and the making of potato-salad, were Johnna's two accomplishments. I remember wishing that I possessed some art like this of Johnna's, for I was always stupid at amusing people, and have always envied those with some little trick or skill to cover a natural lack of parts. Then sometimes, as the guests came or went, we heard the alarm. The bottles were rushed under cover. The proprietor and the bar-tenders scattered upstairs to the hotel. The chain clattered as the inner door was shut, and then we heard the challenge from the patrolman on the street and the rattling of Johnna's door as he tried to get in.

One Sunday, when the bar was full of people, a friend of mine brought in a purser from one of the Cunard steamers. He was one of the thirstiest of men, this purser, with more money than was good for one so thirsty. He had been in the saloon the night before, standing champagne to all comers, with the result that he had had to leave his watch behind as a sort of promise to pay. He had now come to redeem the watch and to stand some more champagne. It chanced that in his apportionment of the drink Johnna received about a pint of champagne, together with a quantity of old Manhattan. The mixture was disastrous, and about half an hour later, when the fusion was complete, he allowed two tall, dark men to enter, neither one of whom was known as a frequenter of the house. It happened that the inner door was open at the moment, for the guard was at

the bar drinking to the purser's health. The
bar was crowded with drinkers. The counter
was littered with champagne bottles. John, the
red-headed bar-tender, was not quite sober. I
had my back turned, and was stacking ice in the
ice-box. The hotel proprietor chanced to see
them as they asked for whisky. "Don't serve
them, John," he cried; but the caution came too
late. John put the four little glasses on the
bar, and gave them the bottle, together with the
jug of ice-water. The other customers, who
had heard the boss's caution, at once guessed
who the two men were. They fell away to right
and left in dead silence. One of them leaned
across to me with a grin. "You're gone up,
my son," he said. "You're pulled for fair."
The two men drank their whisky, and turned to
John and to me. "Put on your coats and come
along," they said. "You're pulled. Where's
the proprietor?" I put on my coat and walked
out to them. John followed, fumbling with his
buttons. The proprietor rose from his chair,
swearing softly at his ill-fortune. He walked
up to the two men and looked at them very
straight, much as a doctor looks at a patient.
The two men looked at him very straight, and

A RAINES LAW ARREST 199

shifted on their feet as though expecting something. John and I, their prisoners, stood waiting to be haled to prison. At last the proprietor spoke. "Say," he said, "won't you come upstairs?" The two men did not answer, but as the boss opened the door they passed out with him. We saw then that they had regulation boots upon their feet, a bit of observation which served me in good stead a few weeks later. "Take off your coats, boys," said one of the drinkers round the bar. "Them cops is on the make. You ain't goin' to be pulled." I took my coat off and went back to my place behind the bar. Almost directly afterwards the electric bell rang from the boss's sitting-room upstairs. I went to see what he wanted, but as I started John called me back to get my tray. "Take a cigar-box with you," he said, "and a packet of cigarettes, and some chew'n' tobacker." So I did as I was bid.

When I got upstairs I found the boss and the two detectives sitting at a table. I put the cigars and other matters on the table, with a box of matches. "Put a quart of champagne on ice and bring it up here," said the boss. "See you don't *frappé* it too cold." So I returned to the bar to cool a bottle, while John sliced a few cucumber sandwiches, put out a little dish of olives and a plate of dry biscuits rather like cheese-stick, of the sort called pretzels. When the wine was cold I decked my tray and bore it in to the trio in their sitting-room. As I entered I saw that one of the detectives was folding up a thick wad of greenbacks which the boss had just handed to him. The other, who probably shared in the money as soon as they reached the police station, had gutted the cigar-box and stored his pockets with twenty-five cent cigars. I put down the wine and poured out three creaming glasses. " Here's happy days," said the boss. " Drink hearty," said one detective. " Let her go, boys," said the other. " Fill them up again," said the boss. " You may go now, John," he added. " Have another pint on ice in case I ring." That was all we heard of the matter. Our case never came before the magistrates.

XXIII

THE SCHOONER-MAN'S CLOSE CALLS

On the Hudson River shore near the railway to Albany there are a number of jetties to which the schooners tie. In the winter when the river is frozen they are deserted, but in the summer and in the spring, when the shad are in the river, they are busy places. They are then alive with fishermen and yachtsmen, and with young men who have come " to go in swimming." The schooners come thither now and again with cargoes of bricks or plank for building. If you are aboard one of the schooners you will find that brick-chucking from man to man, two bricks at a time, is a monotonous employment. It is too like being a figure in a zoetrope. You are very thankful for the dinner hour, when you can sit down with your back to the windlass with a mess of crackerhash upon your knees. It is curious what tales the sailors tell each other during the dinner hour. One man will begin with some anecdote of the last ship he was in, and another will ask, "Was you ever shipwrecked, Bill?" "Why, sure," says Bill, and then out comes the yarn. "Yes," says Bill, "the last ship I was in I got shipwrecked. It was in the Adriatic, going to Tri-East. She was a steamer, one of Cairns Brothers'; the *Morrowdore* her name was. I'd a lot of good clothes, too. I'd everything. Good dungarees and underclothing and a chest. We were going into a bay. It was blowing a bit, but nothing to hurt, and there was a bit of a sea running. It wasn't much, the sea wasn't. The old man got too far in or something. He oughtn't to have been where he was. But we were in ballast. We were very light. So we were running for shelter. I seen them on shore trying to signalize us to warn us off; but the old man didn't see it, or something. And that Mr. Henderson, the second mate, he was mixing paint in the paint locker. He never saw nothing neither. So at last the old man sees something was wrong, and he sings out to me to get a cast of the lead; so I just got in the one cast, and calls out, 'And a half three, sir,' and I was just hauling in to get another throw, and the old man was just ringing the bell to go astern, when she took the reef. She knocked me off my feet; she came on to it fair. So we went speed astern, and let go the anchor; and just as we did that a sea seemed to swing her up and drop her fair on top of it. There we were; we couldn't get her off. We did what we could. But she was there for keeps. Then the sea began to get up, and she began to work and grind. You never felt anything like it. She ripped herself open all along. She tore the bottom off her about three feet all along, so they said. The crowd were all steamer-sailors. They didn't know nothing. Of course I'd been in sail all my life; I didn't think anything of it, but these fellers they were crying out at once. They'd never seen any bad times before. If they'd been in sailing ships, why, they'd 've thought nothing of it. Why, I've seen sailing ships — I've been in 'em, too — But that's enough about them. She ripped her bottom off, about three foot along. She was full to the coamings of the hatches in no time. So then we got up on to the bridge or into the rigging, and they got a rocket along ashore for us, and we all got ashore in the breeches-buoy. It was nothing. But they made such a fuss. They'd never seen any bad times before. If they'd been in sailing ships they'd have thought nothing of it. It wasn't anything to talk of. But I lost all my clothes. I lost my chest, and my bed, and everything. I come ashore with what I stood up in."

" And was that the toughest time you was ever up against? " says another sailor. " No," says Bill, " it was not. I was in a tougher time than that when I first went to sea. I was in a old sailing ship that time — the *Bard of Blaina*. We were going in ballast to New South Wales. Our ballast we'd took in under a tip. It wasn't stowed. I don't know what we didn't have — old walls, old bits of houses, stones, bricks — anything. It was all anyhow, down in the hold. We were very light with it all. We were running down our easting when it happened. The old man had eleven or fifteen pigs aboard. He kept them down in the hold for some reason, so as they'd have room to play about, I guess. He was a queer one, that old man. He took us away down south. We were down in 54 south, for some reason. That'll show you how far south we were — 54 south! The mate said to him, ' Aren't we far enough south, Captain

Chadwick?' 'Ah, go on,' he says, 'I'm going to take you into the cold,' he says. 'I got a lot of warm mitts and flannels in the slop-chest,' he says; 'I want to sell 'em to the hands,' he says; 'so that's why I'm going down into the nice cold weather,' he says. He got it in the neck, too, for going exploring. In the neck he got it.

"One night there come a squall, and that old ship lay over, and her ballast shifted. You can't think what a noise it makes when a stone ballast shifts; it's like being run over by a funeral. Gurrr, it goes. So she lay over on her side, and we never thought she'd right. So the mate he put before it, and then got her round on the other tack and braced up sharp on the other tack, so as to give her a chance. The deck was like the side of a house, or like a s.ooping roof. We had to go down and shift that ballast. We were working there with candles, shovelling and heaving it down. That was a tough time. It was strange about them pigs, too — the captain's eleven or fifteen pigs that I was telling you about. Them pigs had lived in that ballast, and they'd dug themselves burrows just the same as rabbits. And when

we come to shift that ballast we found one of
the pigs got a litter of young ones in her burrow. She'd littered down there in the burrow.
They lived, too, them little ones, until we got
to New South Wales. But you see, in them
parts, in New South Wales, they got a law.
They got a law which won't let you land any
live animals. So when we come to New South
Wales a Government butcher comes off, and
he kills all them pigs of the captain's, and he
lets him keep the meat. He won't let him land
none. So we had a good scoff of pork while it
lasted. There was near on twenty pigs.

"It was a tough time getting that ballast
shifted. We walked on the weather side; I
mean the side that was free, all the passage.
We never expected to get to New South Wales.
The deck was like the side of a house. We
thought she'd go over any time. That was a
tough passage. But one time I'd a narrower
call than that was. I was aboard one of them
Blue Nose ships, what you call a Nova Scotian.
I was mate of her. Of course that don't mean
I'd been to school and passed. It only means
I was the best man aboard her. We were in the
Gulf of St. Lawrence. We were bound for St.

SCHOONER-MAN'S CLOSE CALLS 207

Anns, and it come on foggy. We thought we were all right. We didn't think there was any danger. But there was the fog all about us, white and cold. But we were all right, we thought. We were just slipping slowly ahead for a day or two, and it was foggy all the time. Then we'd a man aboard; one of these land-smellers. And he up to me, and he says, 'We're got in shore. Better go about, mister.' So I ast him why. He says he felt there was land near. So we all laughed. Well, we just kept our course, with everything drawing, and the fog kept on all the time, white and cold, so's you couldn't see the fore-yard. Then, suddenly, there came the 'moo' of a cow, right close alongside. You know how odd sound comes in a fog. That cow might a been a mile away, or it might a been within forty foot. So one of us says, 'A cattleship'; and the land-smeller says, 'Cattle ship up an alley; there's the land.' And just at that very streak the fog lifted, like it will sometimes. It just went. And there was old Shippigan, with the houses and the sun a-shining. I tell you it wasn't more'n a hundred yards off. It was dead ahead. We were running for it with everything drawing. Another ten seconds of time and we'd have been piled up 'all right, all right'; and it wasn't no farmer's place to pile up on, neither. So I just down hellum, and we come round in time. It was a close call. But I'd another narrow call for it, one time. I was in another of them Blue Nose ships. I forgot her name, now. It was the *Odessa* or the *Peninsula*. We were coming home from up by Belle Isle there. It was one spring, and it came on fog. The icebergs and the Gulf Stream is what causes it. It was a white fog, like a Scotch mist. I was on the look-out. I was on the fo'c'sle. It was in the middle watch. So the first thing I saw was a great steamer's smoke-stack away above us. So I sang out, 'Down hellum,' and the lad heard me and jammed it down, and she came up into the wind — lucky for us — and the steamer struck us slantindicular. She mashed our lee bow in, and carried away an anchor and all the head rails. And you should have seen our lee fore rigging. You never saw such a sight. It was an all-night job for all hands, fixing up that little lot. You know what a Blue Nose crew is. It took all hands all night doing that job. However, what was the odds? We'd ought to have been thankful we weren't cut clean across. She'd have got us fair amidships if we'd not put our helm down. We never knew what she was. She just backed clear and vanished. I could just see her green light up above us, and a voice sang out ' My God,' and there she was gone. You see some queer goes at sea. That orficer feller got a turn, I guess. But if you ask me about the sea, I say it ain't a life; not properly it ain't. It's an existence, that's what the sea is. And it's a yaller dawg's existence even at that."

XXIV

THE YARN OF HAPPY JACK

I ONCE knew an old Norwegian sailor, one of the mildest and kindest of men, who attracted me strangely — partly because he was mild and kind, but partly, alas! because he had committed murder. I cannot remember that the crime weighed heavily upon him. He spoke of it frankly, as one would allude to a love affair or the taking of a drink. It was an incident in life. It was part of a day's work. That it was exceptional and reprehensible not one of his friends, I am convinced, imagined.

We made a voyage together, that old Norwegian and I. We were in the same watch, and did very much the same duty. I was very young and green at that time, and he, an old man, a leader in the forecastle, dignified further by poetical circumstance, befriended me in many ways. We used to yarn together in the night watches, under the break of the poop, while the rest of the watch snored heavily in the shadows.

"Hanssen," I asked him one night, "who was Davy Jones?" "Ah, come off with your Davy Jones!" said the boatswain, interrupting. "Look out he don't get you by the leg." I repeated my question. "Davy Jones," said the old man. "I don't know, b'Joe, who Davy Jones was. I know his locker though, b' gee." This was a jest. "Just the sea?" I asked. "Dat's one of 'em, b' gee." "And what's the other?" "You want to know too much, you do," said the boatswain, interrupting us a second time, "you and your Davy Joneses. You're like a Welshman at a fair. 'Who trowned the tuck, Dafy Chones.' Come off with you and give us a breeze." "The other one," said the old man, "it's up in the sky, b' gee." "Is it a sea, too?" I asked. "Of course it is. Didn't you never read your Bible?" "Why, yes, but —" "Well, then, don't you know about the waters above the firm-ment and the waters that are under the firm-ment?" "If you're going to talk Latin," said the boatswain, "I'm sheering off. I'll not rouse no head winds by listenin' to you. Bloody Latin they're talking, them two," he added, to the third mate, as he walked away. "They ought to have been rooks, they'd ought"— by rooks meaning folk in Holy Orders.

After he had gone I got the old man to give me the whole story. He told me that up above, in the sky, there was another sea, of a kind different from our sea, but still fit to carry ships, and much sailed upon by the people of the sky. He told me that the ships were sometimes seen in the air — having perhaps heard from some Greek or Italian of the Fata Morgana, a sort of mirage, which does verily reflect ships in the sky, though I believe upside down. He said that he himself had never seen it, but that it was well known how the anchors from this upper sea carried away chimneys and steeples and broke through roofs in European villages. Such accidents were rather more common in the hills, he added, because the hills made the upper sea shallow. In the valleys, where most big towns are, the water is too deep, and the sky ships do not anchor.

"One time," he said, "there was a sailor. His name, b' gee, was Happy Jack, and he was a big man and a sailor [i.e. he was strong of his body and a good seaman]. One time Happy Jack got paid off and he tink he go home. So he go along a road, and by and by he come to a town, and he found all hands standing in a field looking up. In the middle of the field there was an anchor, and it was like red-hot gold, and the fluke of it was fast in the ground. It was fast to a cable which went up and up into the sky, so far that you couldn't seen the end of it. A great nine-stranded cable it was, with every bit of it shining like gold. It was all laid up of golden rope-yarns. It was a sight to see, that cable and the anchor was. So by and by the parson of the village sings out to get an ax and cut it through, so that they should have the anchor and a bit of the cable to buy new clothes for the poor. So a man goes and comes back with an ax, and he cuts a great chop at it, and the cable just shakes a little, but not so much as a rope-yarn carried away. 'You'll never do it that way,' says Happy Jack; 'you must never have seen a cable, the way you shape at it. What is it you want to do, anyway?' So they said they wanted to get the anchor and the cable to buy new clothes for the poor. 'Well,' says Jack, 'all you got to do is to bury the anchor a fathom deep, and then, when they come to heave in up above, the cable'll carry away, and I shouldn't wonder if you get ten or twenty fathom of it; whereas if you cut it like you're doing you'll not get more'n three feet.' So they asked Jack to show them how. 'It's as simple as kiss,' he says. 'Get spades.' So they got spades. And then they buried the anchor seven or eight feet deep, with rocks and stuff on the top of it, till it was all covered over like it had a house on top. So when they'd done that Happy Jack thinks he'd earned a supper. And the parson says, 'You must be thirsty after all that work.' 'I am thirsty,' he says. So the parson takes him into the town, and gives him a bite of bread and shows him where there's a water-butt. 'Nothing like water,' he says. 'You're right there,' says Jack, 'there isn't.' And so Jack walks out of that town, and back to where the anchor was.

"By and by he began to think that the people in the ship up above might be rather more generous. So he slung his coat off, and began to shinny up the cable, and he climb a great piece; and at last he see the ship.

"And never in his life had he seen a ship the like of that. She was built like of white-hot gold, like a ship built out of the sun — a great shining ship. Her bows was white and round, like a great white cloud, and the air went swirling past them in thin blue eddies. Her ropes were shining, and her blocks were shining, and the sails on her yards were as white as a bow-wash. She had her colours flying at her truck — a long golden steamer that seemed to be white-hot like the hull.

"Now, as he comes up of the sea like, and gets his foot on the cable and his hand on a bobstay, one of the crowd of that ship leans over the rail and looks at him. And he was a queer man, and that's God's truth about him. He hadn't not so much as hair on his head, but instead of hair he had great golden flames. No smoke, mind you, only flames. And he was in a white dress, but the dress was all shining and fiery, and sparks were all over it, like he'd been splashed with them. So Happy Jack kow-tows to this person, and he says, ' You'll have a foul hawse when you come to heave in. They been burying your mud-hook,' he says. So the fiery fellow says, ' Well, Happy Jack, suppose you clear the hawse.' So Jack slides down the cable, and he works all night long, and just as it comes dawn he gets all clear. Then he shinnies up and climbs aboard the ship again.

"Now as soon as he come aboard, the fiery fellows go to the capstan and began to sing, and the song they sang would draw the soul out of the body. It was slow and sweet, and strong and spirited, all in one. And it seemed to Happy Jack that the golden cable was singing too as it came in through the hawseholes. In a few moments the sails were loose and the ship was under way, and she was tearing through it at the rate of knots. All Happy Jack could see was the sails straining, and the ship lying over to it, and the blue air ripping past, and now and then a comet, and a dancing star, and a cloud all red with the sun. So the fiery fellow came up to him, and he says, 'You must be thirsty after all that work.' 'I am thirsty,' he says. So the fiery fellow takes him into the cabin — it was all pictures in the cabin, all blue and green — as pretty as you can't tink. And he give Happy Jack a great golden apple and a bottle of golden wine. And Happy Jack pour out the golden wine and drank it down like it was good for him.

"And the next thing he knew he was lying by the side of the road half a mile from where he lived. And he was in a new suit of clothes with shiny buttons — he was all brass-bound like a reefer. And in his hand there was a bag of golden dollars."

THE END